Gyges

Gyges

By DC Fidler

Published by DCFidler Publishing

2021

Published by DCFidler Publishing
1117 University Avenue, #505
Morgantown, WV 26505
DCFidlerpublishing@gmail.com

Printed in the United States of America
by Kindle Direct Publishing

10, 9, 8, 7, 6, 5, 4, 3, 2, 1

Front cover: Etty, W. (1830). *Candaules, King of Lydia, Shews his Wife by Stealth to Gyges, One of his Ministers, as She Goes to Bed* [Oil on canvas]. Tate Britain. Public Domain
Back cover: Fidler, D. (1972). *Last Twilight* [Oil on canvas]. DC Fidler Collection. © Donald Carl Fidler

ISBN: 979-8-9852256-5-5 (paperback)
ISBN: 979-8-9852256-6-2 (ebook)

Appreciation

Thank you to Sandi Constantino-Thompson and David Beech for detailed critiques on early drafts.

Thank you to M.T. Pockets Theatre, WVU School of Theatre and Dance, RJ Casey, and Travis Teffner for collaborating with me on creating plays and screenplays, sharing invaluable moments of imagining and writing.

Setting

The year is 2015. The location is Norfolk, Virginia.

Scenes take place in Dr. Vivien Heifetz's home/office.

1. Basement Laboratory that also serves as Timothy's bedroom. The lab area has a gurney, stools, table with computer monitor, and an IV tree with solution bag and tubing. Timothy's sleeping area consists of a simple cot or mattress with a pillow, a blanket, and a folding chair. Often the portable rabbit cage is in the room on the floor.
2. Vivien's Medical Office with an exam table, a small table with a computer monitor, a small file cabinet, and stools for Vivien and patients to sit upon.
3. Vivien's Waiting Room with three or four chairs, a small cabinet in which to place towels, and a waste basket.

Scenes also take place in Evan and Paige's home.

4. Living Room with a couch, an end table with small lamp, chairs, and a coffee table.

Special Note:

Since characters can take over other characters' bodies, characters are identified by the bodies they inhabit at the moment.

Maximum sets:

Whatever artists can imagine and afford.

Minimalist set suggestions:

A minimum of furniture and props can be used so that the focus is on the actors. Scenes can be staged in limbo with the center stage lit and the side and upstage edges in the dark. Simple furniture such as folding chairs can sit in dark areas and be slid into lit areas when called upon.

There can be an upstage screen for actors to change costume behind. When not in a scene, actors can sit on the periphery of the stage.

Actors can mime opening, walking through, closing, slamming, and knocking on doors. Actors can mime looking at photos and looking at themselves in mirrors.

Stools can be draped with a sheet to represent an exam table, and folding chairs can be used for furniture. Side-by-side chairs can be draped with a cover to represent a couch. Fake cardboard computers and monitors similar to those in furniture stores can be used.

Timothy can stand on a black box when peering in Evan and Paige's window.

Props

- Hand-held monitor (A small external computer drive can suffice)
- Two computers
- Various drinking glasses
- Lab notebooks
- Necklace with key
- Children's story book
- File cabinet
- File folder with papers
- Nail file
- Waste basket
- Fake dog under sheet
- Portable rabbit cage
- Small bag of carrots
- Sandwiches
- Stack of hand towels
- Package of 2x2 gauze
- Laptop
- Envelopes
- Nasal spray bottle
- Landline phone
- Mixing bowl with spoon
- Compact disc
- Small medicine package
- Antique book
- Box with small camping items
- Mobile phones
- Clip board with paper
- Portable external computer drive
- Bloody cloth
- Arm bandage
- Syringe
- IV tree with solution bag and tubing
- Makeup case
- Backpack
- Tarp
- Knapsack

Characters

Dr. Vivien Heifetz –Age 60. She is a neurologist and computer engineer. She never married and never dates. She lives in a three-room apartment above her struggling pain clinic. She no longer has a medical license. She spends much time doing unfunded, independent research. Seven years ago, she accepted a thirteen-year-old boy, Timothy, into her home. She has a slight German accent that is stronger with words such as her name. She attended a strict boarding school and her parents were well educated. This resulted in her learning formal language such as using relatively few contractions, split infinitives, and split compound verbs. When she becomes excited her grammar slightly deteriorates.

Timothy Daniels – Age 20. Lives with Vivien. Timothy was abandoned as an infant on the steps of St. Mary's Catholic Home for Children with Disabilities. When he was thirteen years old, Vivien accepted him into her home. Timothy has injuries that resulted from a traumatic birth that left him with a marked right-leg limp, limited use of his right arm, and lack of sensation in his pelvic area. He is self-conscious about his disabilities and rarely leaves the house. He has poor social skills but has genius-level cognitive skills. He was home schooled by various tutors Vivien hired. He often smells objects, a trait of some people with Asperger's Syndrome on the autistic spectrum. He smells food before taking the first bite as if making certain it is safe.

Paige Buchanan – Age 28. She has been married to Evan Buchanan for eleven months. She is a fashion magazine photographer. She has headaches and is a patient of Dr. Heifetz.

Evan Buchanan – Age 29. He has been married to Paige Buchanan for eleven months. He works as a junior partner in a large investment firm. He has unremitting tingling in his left foot from a combat injury in Iraq. He often lifts his left foot and rotates it and rubs it. He always has a two-to-three-day growth of beard - well trimmed

Brittany Hickman – Age 17. She is a high school senior at a School of the Arts, studying ballet. She is also a patient of Dr. Heifetz. She dresses in clothes more appropriate for an older avant-garde fashion model. She always wears a wrist band on her left wrist, believing her left wrist is overly large.

GYGES

ACT ONE - Scene One

Setting: Laboratory/Timothy's bedroom at night. A spot rises on a small rabbit cage on the floor. Seconds later, TIMOTHY carries a notebook and a small bag of carrots as he hobbles from a dark portion of the room to the cage, prompting stage lights to full. He is wearing only old-man-style briefs. His right arm is barely functional. He struggles to kneel and talk to rabbit.

TIMOTHY: Wake up, Perseus. Carrot time.

(He unlatches and latches the cage flip latch three times, opens door, kisses his fingers, reaches in to touch rabbit, and smells fingers.)

TIMOTHY: Aunt Vivien is running late. Migraine. Lights, sounds, smells, all kinds of junk trigger her headaches. In the Tenth Century, Ali Ibn would have strapped a dead mole on her head. Wouldn't you love to see Vivien with a mole stuck to her head? Nineteenth Century? Electrified baths. Between you and me, I'd be first in line to throw the switch. *(Makes electric zap sound)* More carrot, buddy?

(He feeds a bite of carrot to Perseus)

TIMOTHY: I taught you yesterday CGRP triggers migraines. So, you know what this is? *(Displaying page of notebook)* My design. Little gold nanoparticles, like microscopic strategic missiles, stop CGRP dead in its tracks.

(He makes an explosive noise)

TIMOTHY: Vivien won't even read my migraine research. Stuck on using her deadly IV drugs for deep sleep. They'll kill her one day. *(Feeds more carrot to Perseus)* Tomorrow, I'm refining a nasal aerosol. Shoot nano-sensors and transmitters up the nose to the brain in transgenic mice. No rabbits.

VIVIEN: *(Yells offstage)* Timothy? Safe to come in?

TIMOTHY: Just a minute.

(TIMOTHY closes cage and hides notebook under bed)

TIMOTHY: Okay.

(VIVIEN enters, carrying a notebook. She sees TIMOTHY in boxer shorts and shields her eyes.)

VIVIEN: Mein Gott. Put on some clothes.

TIMOTHY: Oh. Right.

(He awkwardly dresses in pajama bottoms, struggling with his almost-useless right arm and limp leg. VIVIEN averts her eyes as she waits. TIMOTHY climbs into bed and holds up a children's story book.)

TIMOTHY: Ready for my story.

VIVIEN: You think you earned a story?

TIMOTHY: Cleaned eighty-three mice cages.

VIVIEN: A children's story. Mein Gott. You are twenty years old.

TIMOTHY: You always say that when you are tired.

VIVIEN: I say that when you are ridiculous.

TIMOTHY: Ursula adored reading to me.

VIVIEN: I paid Ursula to tutor you in physics, not climb in your bed to read to you.

TIMOTHY: She was very friendly.

VIVIEN: I have no doubt.

TIMOTHY: After this year, we can stop.

VIVIEN: When I was twenty, I went out with friends. Movies. Dancing. Room-temp German beer—in moderation of course.

TIMOTHY: I have Perseus.

VIVIEN: Mein Gott. No one takes a rabbit to a movie or tavern.

TIMOTHY: I promise, I'll make friends.

(VIVIEN opens her notebook as if reading)

VIVIEN: Once upon a time—

TIMOTHY: —That's your lab book.

VIVIEN: Once upon a time there were bedtime stories of pigs building houses.

TIMOTHY: Straw and sticks and—

VIVIEN: —And wolves eating little girls.

TIMOTHY: And grandmothers.

VIVIEN: And doctors bringing the dead to life.

TIMOTHY: Victor Frankenstein.

VIVIEN: Bedtime stories about sorcerers with empowered cloaks.

TIMOTHY: Harry my buddy Potter!

VIVIEN: But did you know there are mischievous mysteries occurring this very day and time?

TIMOTHY: Yuk. A patient story.

VIVIEN: A science story. More enchanting than your Harry Potter.

TIMOTHY: I want magic.

VIVIEN: There was a doctor, a neurologist.

TIMOTHY: A woman neurologist?

VIVIEN: Doesn't matter.

TIMOTHY: Is she also a computer engineer?

VIVIEN: Doesn't matter.

TIMOTHY: In her 60s, never married?—No more stories about you!

VIVIEN: For years this brilliant researcher dreamed of traveling into the bodies of other people.

TIMOTHY: What? No one can do that.

VIVIEN: But woodsmen can cut people out of wolves' bellies? Please. This charming neurologist—

TIMOTHY: —Charming?

VIVIEN: Neurologist slash engineer wanted to experience what it felt like to be inside of other humans.

TIMOTHY: Spy on their thinking?

VIVIEN: Thoughts are private, sacred. She wanted to know what it felt like to walk, to sit, to lie inside others' bodies. How bad is the back pain, the cramps, the tingling?

TIMOTHY: She's a physician. She can ask.

VIVIEN: Experience how other people treat them.

TIMOTHY: Just ask!

VIVIEN: People lie to the world. To themselves. More than anything in her life, the doctor wanted to expand the possibilities of medical science beyond the imaginable.

TIMOTHY: Will this story have conflict?

VIVIEN: Have I ever told you a lame bedtime story?

TIMOTHY: Tell it loud enough for Perseus to hear.

VIVIEN: No timid rabbit could tolerate so much conflict.

TIMOTHY: That much build-up means it's a boring patient story.

VIVIEN: Patient stories are bragging stories. Accomplishments. Like when you brag about inventing computer programs.

TIMOTHY: You couldn't do your research without my programs.

VIVIEN: This story has every bit as much conflict as *Frankenstein* or *Dracula*.

TIMOTHY: People get burned or staked?

VIVIEN: It's the continuation of last week's story.

TIMOTHY: The queen's squire adding magic flowers to her drink for sleep. Giving her bioengineered mushrooms to wake her. Like I don't know what that symbolizes. I want a story not made up about you and me. I want dragons and space ships and—

VIVIEN: —It was easier to tell stories when you were younger.

TIMOTHY: At least have her use the magic flowers to put elephants or dragons to sleep.

VIVIEN: Do I get to tell this story or do you want to tell it?

TIMOTHY: We tell stories together.

VIVIEN: *(Sighs)* Our modus operandi. Once upon a time—

TIMOTHY: —Or present time.

VIVIEN: Once upon a time ...

End of Scene

GYGES

Scene Two

Setting: Vivien's medical office in day. PAIGE is sitting on an exam table. VIVIEN sprays aerosol in PAIGE's nostrils.

VIVIEN: There. Simple.

(VIVIEN hands a small hand-held monitor to PAIGE, who examines it closely. VIVIEN studies her computer screen.)

VIVIEN: In a matter of minutes, nano-chips in the aerosol will begin attaching in your brain.

PAIGE: I already feel like a freak. Now my brain will be stuffed with computer chips.

VIVIEN: You won't notice any effect.

(PAIGE shakes her head in doubt)

VIVIEN: Even microbiologists cannot see the chips under microscopes. Those little receptor-targeted nanoparticles will perform quietly.

PAIGE: I'm a robot.

VIVIEN: Not even close. Thursday night, 9 p.m., turn on your monitor. The chips and I will do the rest.

PAIGE: Should I lie or sit?

VIVIEN: Whatever is best to relax your mind.

(PAIGE suddenly shivers and hides her face)

VIVIEN: Is something wrong?

(PAIGE sheepishly shakes her head "no")

VIVIEN: That monitor will convey information to my computers. We'll talk on Monday. The talking is essential.

PAIGE: What if you find a tumor?

VIVIEN: You do not have a tumor. We are studying sensations of pressure, pain, emotions.

PAIGE: Can I leave the house? Walk outside?

VIVIEN: The monitor relies on your home Wi-Fi. Remain inside from 9 p.m. to morning.

PAIGE: Better than those CAT scans Doctor Ferguson tortured me with. I got claustrophobic.

VIVIEN: This is easier.

PAIGE: What are the true chances this will help my headaches?

VIVIEN: Excellent. Leave the monitor on until morning to transmit enough data. While you were in Cancun how were your headaches?

PAIGE: No headaches.

VIVIEN: Interesting.

PAIGE: I was alone photographing Elle spring fashions. Evan couldn't get away from his firm.

VIVIEN: He's a junior partner in his investment firm, up for promotion in April, right?

PAIGE: How do you know that?

VIVIEN: Your initial assessment questionnaire.

PAIGE: I can't believe you remember that. You must be a genius.

VIVIEN: My father insisted my step-brother and I persistently exercised our memories.

PAIGE: I should take lessons. Last night I ran my fourth cell phone through the washer.

VIVIEN: Mein Gott. This monitor is a marvel, but it cannot survive agitated, soapy water.

PAIGE: I will be careful.

VIVIEN: Expensive.

PAIGE: I read the directions. Then lost them.

VIVIEN: I'll print another copy.

PAIGE: Evan made a copy for me on his phone.

VIVIEN: Any chance Evan will come in, allow me to treat his combat injury?

PAIGE: He prefers numbing his foot tingling with his little recreation habit.

VIVIEN: Habit?

PAIGE: Snorting coke. Nothing I can do.

VIVIEN: Cocaine will exacerbate his problems. How did you get that bruise on your arm?

PAIGE: Uh … Bumped it on the car door probably.

VIVIEN: You've been married a year, correct?

PAIGE: Eleven months.

VIVIEN: How did you two meet?

PAIGE: Cayman Islands. My sister's wedding. The animals you tested did fine, right?

VIVIEN: Brilliant results. When we pinched their claws their brains registered pain, awake or asleep.

PAIGE: Did pain look different when they were asleep from when they were awake?

VIVIEN: You have quite the scientific mind, Mrs. Buchanan. When they were awake, their brains also registered panic. When they were being fed, joy with less pain. The degree of pain is determined by meanings we assign to pain.

PAIGE: My pain is not imagined.

VIVIEN: No, no. Not imagined. But meanings alter the quality. Example: my colleagues had students dip hands into buckets filled with ice and water. All students experienced pain and within thirty seconds jerked out their hands. Next, they assigned half to concentrate on the ice and half to concentrate on sexual photographs—tasteful sexual photographs. Which group tolerated pain longer?

PAIGE: That's a no brainer.

VIVIEN: Forty-seven-thousand dollars for science to confirm the obvious.

PAIGE: So in Cancun, because I was not fretting over the house, not fretting over meals—

VIVIEN: —Information you know. But we will uncover information you do not know.

PAIGE: Maybe I'm better off not knowing.

VIVIEN: We hope for surprises. I learned the color orange causes me anxiety.

PAIGE: You tested yourself?

VIVIEN: Orange like the school bus I rode in first grade, when Jeremy Higgins and Ben Caldwell teased me. Made fun of my German accent and ears so much I got into trouble at school for refusing to speak or remove my hat. School-bus orange makes me anxious. Helpful information.

PAIGE: I bet those guys grew up to be thugs.

VIVIEN: Jeremy became a NASA engineer and Ben is a Chicago Tribune editorialist. Or so my step-brother wrote me.

PAIGE: Do you keep up with them?

VIVIEN: My family sent me off to a strict boarding school. I became a methodical recluse. Now I live in three small rooms above this clinic.

PAIGE: A mad scientist recluse.

(She has an outburst of energetic laughter. Vivien remains serious, prompting PAIGE to silence.)

VIVIEN: I trust not "mad."

PAIGE: No, not "mad." I didn't mean to insult you. Just making a … Sorry.

VIVIEN: Okay then. Thursday night I'll study your brain on my computer. Monday we'll talk in person. Do not drown my monitor in your washing machine.

(She exits as PAIGE sits a moment and looks at monitor)

PAIGE: Don't hurt me little black box.

End of Scene

GYGES

Scene Three

Setting: Laboratory/Timothy's bedroom at night. TIMOTHY is sitting on the floor, wearing pajamas. VIVIEN is sitting in a bedside chair, reading from her notebook.

VIVIEN: And the woman left the doctor's office, monitor in tow. Okay, time for sleep. No poor-poor Timothy stories to stall.

TIMOTHY: That woman won't use the monitor. She mistrusts her doctor.

VIVIEN: She wants to be rid of headaches.

TIMOTHY: This isn't spectacular. Same way you monitor mice.

(He hobbles to cage and talks as he checks the flip latch, unlatching and latching it three times)

VIVIEN: And monitor chimpanzees.

TIMOTHY: We don't have chimpanzees.

VIVIEN: At the university lab.

TIMOTHY: Someone else knows about our work?

VIVIEN: The four lab technicians I am helping to tutor.

TIMOTHY: Oh. You never mention them.

VIVIEN: Mentioning them makes you feel bad about fearing to go out in public. I tell them very little about your and my work. They must prove themselves before I trust them.

TIMOTHY: And the doctor tells the woman very little.

VIVIEN: Like surgeons. No reason to scare patients with gory details.

TIMOTHY: There's more. I knew it, I knew it. Give me a hint.

VIVIEN: The reality is ...

TIMOTHY: *(Pause)* I'm waiting.

VIVIEN: The doctor ... *(Pause)*

TIMOTHY: Oh, for gosh sakes.

VIVIEN: The doctor will roughly SEE what the patient sees. Roughly HEAR what the patient hears. Feel warmth and cold, taste pepper and salt, smell magnolias and dog poop, feel sweat trickling down her forehead, feel palpitations and toes being pinched too tightly in ridiculous high heels.

TIMOTHY: Holy moly! She's going into the woman's brain.

VIVIEN: Exploring the woman's perceptions.

TIMOTHY: How can the doctor do that?

VIVIEN: The doctor's brain will house a Nano-Chip Two, performing as a receptor.

TIMOTHY: Holy moly. Is that sci fi or real?

VIVIEN: The computer will convey information from the woman's brain to the monitor, to the computer, to the doctor's brain.

TIMOTHY: Can the doctor read the woman's thoughts?

VIVIEN: Thoughts are sacred. Not to be touched.

TIMOTHY: Because that would be peering into her soul. This has chances for HUGE conflict!

VIVIEN: If not for the fine doctor's purity of heart.

TIMOTHY: People get tempted. Give me a hint of what's to come.

VIVIEN: Perhaps one day, the doctor will be able to direct subjects' behaviors. Now go to sleep.

TIMOTHY: You always do this to me.

VIVIEN: I have no idea what you mean.

TIMOTHY: Of course, you do. You set me up to believe all is simple and good and then WHAM!

VIVIEN: You confuse the way I tell stories with the way the nuns at St. Mary's orphanage told you stories.

TIMOTHY: Nuns never set me up.

VIVIEN: All Bible stories set up people. I'll tell you more Tuesday.

TIMOTHY: This is Wednesday.

VIVIEN: Six days.

(TIMOTHY talks as he walks to cage and checks latch three times and sniffs his fingers)

TIMORTHY: In our lab, why do you put some mice to sleep but not others?

VIVIEN: A sleeping mouse is in a dream state. Unaware of its environment. That frees its brain to sync with the computer. Perceptions and sensations of the awake mouse transfer to the monitor, to the computer, and flood into the sleeping mouse's brain.

TIMOTHY: So, the sleeping mouse has the receptor chip?

VIVIEN: Perceiving, sensing the awake mouse's body sensations. Using your brain-syncing program.

TIMOTHY: So … it's like the sleeping mouse dreams its way into the awake mouse.

VIVIEN: Uh … Strange way to put it.

TIMOTHY: Holy moly. *(Pause)* Maybe in the story, the doctor can go into a patient's mind but not be able to come back out. Get stuck.

VIVIEN: All mice and chimpanzees came back fine. I did it with a mouse and a dog.

TIMOTHY: Holy moly. Think if they could talk. Tell us their experience.

VIVIEN: Maybe one day researchers will sync an animal brain with a human brain.

TIMOTHY: The gods would destroy them for violating nature's laws.

VIVIEN: People once thought that about humans trying to fly.

TIMOTHY: You are not allowed to mess with Perseus's brain.

VIVIEN: Mein Gott. When I select an animal, it will be a noble animal.

TIMOTHY: I'm moving him closer to my bed so you don't screw up his brain.

VIVIEN: Look how plump you made it.

TIMOTHY: You derive cruel pleasure making me wait for endings to stories.

(She snaps her fingers and points at bed)

TIMOTHY: So unfair.

VIVIEN: Life is unfair.

TIMOTHY: My life is unfair.

VIVIEN: Goodnight, Timothy.

(VIVIEN walks toward the door but is stopped)

TIMOTHY: Vivien?

VIVIEN: Goodnight, Timothy.

TIMOTHY: In my books, families tell bedtime stories and then kiss their children goodnight.

VIVIEN: I'm a German fairy-tale old woman. I do not hug. I do not kiss. Besides, you are twenty.

TIMOTHY: But when I was younger?

VIVIEN: Goodnight.

TIMOTHY: The nuns never kissed me at bedtime. They resented me.

VIVIEN: Why would you think that?

TIMOTHY: Because my drug-dealing mother dumped me off in a basket on their steps.

VIVIEN: Who told you such a grotesque fairytale?

TIMOTHY: Sister Sarah yelled that at me when I wet my pants. Sister Agnes told her I didn't have feeling in my pelvic area, that sometimes I have accidents, but Sister Sarah kept yelling and saying I was cursed and too expensive for any mother to care for and that my damaged body was the reason my mother started dealing drugs.

VIVIEN: Sister Sarah sounds like a witch. Your mother may have taken medications, but she certainly was no drug dealer.

TIMOTHY: Sister Agnes said my mother was fantastically beautiful and intelligent.

VIVIEN: I'm sure she was correct.

TIMOTHY: Do you think I'll ever find her?

VIVIEN: I am blessed those gracious nuns at St. Mary's gave you to me. Now goodnight

TIMOTHY: Maybe she came looking for me after you took me out.

VIVIEN: The nuns raised you for thirteen years. Their hearts broke when I volunteered to raise you.

TIMOTHY: They refused to tell me who my mother was.

VIVIEN: Nuns honor secrets.

TIMOTHY: Wouldn't tell me her name, not my birth date so I could search online. Sister Sarah said I was born under a bridge. How do I even know my name is real?

VIVIEN: Your bedtime stalling strategies haven't worked the past seven years. They won't work tonight.

(She snaps fingers, points at bed, and walks toward the door)

TIMOTHY: Wait, really wait! I don't want to give you herbs for deep sleep anymore. I have terrible attention. I may slip and kill you.

VIVIEN: Your attention is frightful. But I require deep sleep when I have migraines.

TIMOTHY: I can design a timer to automate your "herbs."

VIVIEN: *(Talking while standing in doorway)* Automate? Clever. Now, allow me to get my rest or there will be no next chapter.

TIMOTHY: If the woman patient has no idea the doctor is visiting her brain, that's wrong.

VIVIEN: You asked for conflict.

TIMOTHY: Make sure Perseus's cage is locked.

VIVIEN: You checked his cage three times three.

(As soon as VIVIEN closes door, TIMOTHY walks to cage, checks the latch three times, and smells his fingers)

TIMOTHY: You're a lucky bunny I keep Vivien away from you. She would starve you to death. Or dissect your liver and brain. My real mother would feed you. Let you play outside.

(He kisses Perseus's cage door and climbs in bed)

TIMOTHY: I like stories with conflict ... But conflict makes my mind race.

(He pulls covers over his head, pauses, tosses off covers, and sits up)

TIMOTHY: I'll work on the timer.

End of Scene

GYGES

Scene 4

Setting: Vivien's medical office in day. BRITTANY is sitting on exam table as VIVIEN stands before her.

BRITTANY: I spotted your flyer on the bulletin board at Joyce's Organic Soap'N'Stuff. "Treatments for unusual and annoying pain."

VIVIEN: What is annoying you?

BRITTANY: My left wrist. Astronomically annoying. It's larger than my right wrist.

(She holds out her left wrist. VIVIEN examines BRITTANY'S left wrist and then her right wrist.)

VIVIEN: Hm ... They appear equal.

BRITTANY: Obviously they are not.

VIVIEN: Is it painful?

BRITTANY: It's annoying. I can't take pain medications. They interfere with my ballet technique.

VIVIEN: I do not believe in traditional medicines.

BRITTANY: That's what your flyer said.

VIVIEN: Did you injure your wrist?

BRITTANY: I was born with a weird wrist. I tried ice packs, heat packs, stretch exercises, splints, ointments with arnica, massage, flaxseed, turmeric, magnesium, yoga. Acupuncture's next. And I'm not a computer geek, so it's not carpal tunnel. Your flyer said, "Non-traditional." Are you a medical doctor? You don't have "M.D." on your office sign.

VIVIEN: I attended medical school, yes, but I abandoned the medical profession.

BRITTANY: Good. I'm so about non-conformity.

VIVIEN: Describe this "annoying" feeling.

BRITTANY: A conforming-type M.D. diagnosed me as depressed. I assure you I am anything but.

VIVIEN: Describe "annoying."

BRITTANY: You know when you want something really, really bad? And you'll die if you don't get it? But you don't? Your stomach sinks, churns, feels hollow. My wrist annoys me that way. Lots of famous people have interesting sensations.

VIVIEN: Their bodies talked to them and they listened.

BRITTANY: Exactly! Thank God I found someone who understands.

VIVIEN: *(Examining BRITTANY's hands)* How often do you think about your wrist?

BRITTANY: Twenty-five hours a day.

VIVIEN: There are people who have Raynaud's Disorder. Attacks of super cold hands and feet. Not enough blood in their fingers and toes. They get blisters. I instruct them to imagine hot sun and toasty fires. Like magic, they warm.

BRITTANY: Holy shit. Excuse me.

VIVIEN: Your left hand is excessively warm. Your right hand is cool.

BRITTANY: My left wrist is always hot.

VIVIEN: Maybe because you concentrate on it "twenty-five hours a day."

BRITTANY: I have to!

VIVIEN: I want to have you sniff a spray that will enable your brain to send signals to my computer. Learn your body's sensations, emotions, how you perceive your world.

BRITTANY: That's so cool! Wait! My non-creative, totally conforming mother will never agree.

VIVIEN: How old are you?

BRITTANY: Seventeen.

VIVIEN: In another year you can choose what you want to do with your own body.

BRITTANY: Boy does that describe me to a tee. I do exactly what I want with my own body. Like my mom didn't want me to dance. I mean really? What the shit does she know, right? So not creative. Boring.

VIVIEN: I doubt you are boring.

BRITTANY: Hey! We only have one life, one body.

End of Scene

GYGES

Scene 5

Setting: Evan and Paige's living room at night. EVAN examines the hand-held monitor as PAIGE arranges pillows on the couch and then lies on her back. Several times, EVAN lifts his left foot and rubs it.

EVAN: Your quack's black box is crap. Snake oil. She's dazzling you with carnie-fortune-teller stories and charging us a fortune.

PAIGE: Nothing else worked. She offered to treat your foot.

EVAN: Shit no.

PAIGE: She wrote a research paper.

EVAN: Did she publish it?

(PAIGE shrugs)

EVAN: Cause her ideas are bullshit. Like the VA's idea to treat us combat soldiers with video games.

PAIGE: You said that helped.

EVAN: I said blowing up crap was cool. Didn't help my foot worth shit.

PAIGE: Hand me my monitor.

(EVAN hands monitor to PAIGE. She turns it on.)

EVAN: If that little black box worked, the military would use it to interrogate terrorists.

PAIGE: Reason to keep it out of their hands.

EVAN: She's a con artist, Paige. She doesn't even have a fucking license on her wall.

PAIGE: I said I don't recall seeing it. It's nine p.m. I'm attempting to relax my mind. So, quit antagonizing me.

EVAN: What if that thing electrocutes you?

PAIGE: I'm not connected to it. It sends signals through our Wi-Fi. Better than sticking my head in another pulsating machine. Dr. Heifetz said I'll have amnesia for this.

EVAN: Good. I'll unload my darkest secrets—since you won't remember.

PAIGE: I know your darkest secrets.

EVAN: Yeah, right. The guys in my unit took an oath. We don't talk about Iraq.

PAIGE: College secrets.

EVAN: College?

PAIGE: Fraternity gang bang.

EVAN: Fraternity what???

PAIGE: Amanda's wedding in the Cayman Islands. You were drunk and slurred out a confession.

EVAN: I would never—

(PAIGE suddenly sits up, dazed, hardly moves, and whispers in a mild German accent similar to Vivien's speech. She looks around room with amazement.)

PAIGE: Mein Gott.

EVAN: What did you say?

PAIGE: *(Flat affect)* This is strange.

EVAN: What's strange?

PAIGE: Oh, hi Mr. ... Evan. The sensations. Clearer than I expected. It's like being here.

EVAN: I'm turning off that damn contraption.

(He picks up monitor)

PAIGE: No! ... I'm fine. Just ... disoriented.

EVAN: That's not okay.

PAIGE: It's momentary.

EVAN: I don't trust Dr. Heifetz.

PAIGE: I ... She tested this procedure on dozens of lab animals.

EVAN: Not humans.

PAIGE: It works. *(Chuckles)* It works spectacularly.

EVAN: No headache?

PAIGE: Exactly how I thought I would feel sharing brain functions ... I am starved!

EVAN: Even if for a second you are not okay, I'll rip that fucking thing apart. Stomp it to bits.

(PAIGE walks around the room, examining objects)

PAIGE: Ingenious.

EVAN: *(Pause)* So ... When I was drunk, what did I say about the gang bang?

PAIGE: The what?

EVAN: My fraternity. Two minutes ago, you said—

PAIGE: —Uh ... I don't remember. The monitoring. Amnesia.

EVAN: Freaky.

PAIGE: Dr. Heifetz said to expect short-term memory loss.

EVAN: Say your doctor's name again.

PAIGE: Heifetz.

EVAN: Why are you pronouncing her name with a German accent?

PAIGE: How do I usually pronounce it?

EVAN: Heifetz.

PAIGE: I want to show respect, pronounce her name correctly.

EVAN: All of your words sound different.

(PAIGE examines her hands and arms. She rubs the palm of one hand over opposite arm.)

PAIGE: Nice. Smooth.

(She walks to mirror, looks at herself, touches her face)

PAIGE: My skin is young.

EVAN: You're weirding me out.

PAIGE: Colors are different.

EVAN: I'm turning that fucker off.

(He reaches for the monitor but PAIGE yells and snaps her fingers)

PAIGE: Don't touch that!

EVAN: Jesus! What? This "thing" makes you scream at me?

PAIGE: I want desperately to be rid of my headaches.

EVAN: "Desperately?" *(Tender)* Okay. We'll do this together. Come here.

(He motions for PAIGE to come to him. She hesitantly walks to him. He hugs her and she becomes uncomfortable and squirms.)

EVAN: What's the matter?

PAIGE: I need to go to the toilet.

EVAN: Toilet? The bathroom?

PAIGE: Bathroom. Toilet.

EVAN: I told you to quit drinking so much water.

(PAIGE stands, uncertain which way to go. EVAN pauses to watch.)

EVAN: Are you going or not? Don't tell me you have amnesia for where the guest bathroom is.

PAIGE: No. I feel a bit unsteady.

EVAN: Take my hand.

(He guides PAIGE to the door and opens it for her. She steps partially into doorway.)

PAIGE: That's far enough. I can take it from here.

EVAN: I'll stand with you, make sure you don't fall.

PAIGE: No! *(Calms)* Thank you.

(She closes the door. Evan pauses a moment, goes to phone and calls, keeping his voice low.)

EVAN: Mom? Paige started that headache monitor thing I told you about. She's acting strange ... Three minutes ago. She's gotta do it for an hour ... Well, her voice, her accent is different. She said colors look different. She keeps feeling her skin. Real creepy.

(PAIGE opens the door and sticks her head out)

PAIGE: Evan? There is no hand towel.

EVAN: Where you insist we keep them. Bottom left drawer, little green dresser thing.

PAIGE: Looks blue.

(PAIGE closes the door. EVAN speaks into the phone.)

EVAN: Mom? I don't trust this.

End of Scene

GYGES

Scene 6

Setting: Laboratory/Timothy's bedroom in day. VIVIEN sips a fruit drink while TIMOTHY eats a sandwich and sips a milkshake. He smells sandwich before each bite.

VIVIEN: The aging doctor did not count on touching her skin and discovering it to be smooth, not wrinkled, not tissue-paper-thin. New like a child's skin.

TIMOTHY: She touches young patients' skin in her clinic.

VIVIEN: Not from the inside. Not as if the skin were her own. And the colors! Dazzling. Everything had a blue tint. Scientists have never been certain if different brains interpret the color spectrum differently. They do.

(TIMOTHY walks to cage, spills splash of milkshake on floor, and awkwardly cleans spill with his left sleeve. He tears off a bite of sandwich and sticks bite into cage.)

TIMOTHY: Here you go, Perseus.

VIVIEN: Don't feed your sandwich to that creature.

TIMOTHY: He loves my carrot and mayonnaise sandwiches. And milkshakes. Don't you boy?

VIVIEN: You have no idea what mayonnaise or chocolate may do to a rabbit.

TIMOTHY: Did the woman sense smells differently?

VIVIEN: The doctor did not report smells. Maybe the woman has an impaired sense of smell.

TIMOTHY: The doctor should put her into someone else's brain. Perseus could teach her about smells, couldn't you boy?

VIVIEN: Interesting theory.

TIMOTHY: You can't use Perseus! Hands off! How soon will the doctor visit the woman's brain?

VIVIEN: Thursday evening.

TIMOTHY: Same night you usually have migraines and demand deep sleep. Can the doctor help the woman's headaches?

VIVIEN: What is your hypothesis?

TIMOTHY: Where and when does the woman develop headaches?

VIVIEN: At home.

TIMOTHY: What's her home like?

VIVIEN: Small. Lovely.

TIMOTHY: Larger than our three rooms?

VIVIEN: It's a house. It's larger.

TIMOTHY: I want to live in a house. Not sleep in a makeshift bedroom in a basement laboratory.

VIVIEN: One day. The woman did not have one headache while the doctor hosted her.

TIMOTHY: "Hosted?" That's creepy. If the woman stays in her house, the doctor can't learn much.

VIVIEN: Limits of science.

TIMOTHY: Her monitor is programmed to send data through her home Wi-Fi, right?

VIVIEN: Correct.

TIMOTHY: The doctor should alter the software, send data through the woman's mobile phone network. Then the woman can go anywhere.

VIVIEN: Would that be difficult?

TIMOTHY: Please. An eight-year-old could program it. I'll tinker with your software. But networks go down. What happens if there's a break in transmission?

VIVIEN: The doctor goes back to her brain. The patient reclaims her brain. No harm.

TIMOTHY: Why doesn't the doctor have amnesia?

VIVIEN: The doctor's brain is not hijacked. Even though

asleep, it remains dominant.

TIMOTHY: "Hijacked." Even creepier. I'll tinker with your software after lunch.

VIVIEN: You are amazing, Timothy Daniels.

(She walks toward door)

VIVIEN: The Bill Gates of medical computers.

TIMOTHY: Bill Gates can walk, run—probably juggle. He has feeling in his crotch.

VIVIEN: (*Pause)* That's sad you were born without sensation down below ... You have a brilliant mind, Timothy. Cherish that gift ... Do you want me to heat up some stew?

TIMOTHY: Perseus does.

VIVIEN: No more human food for that chubby fur ball.

(She exits. TIMOTHY resumes feeding Perseus.)

TIMOTHY: No worries. I won't let that woman steal your soul. I'm twenty now. Old enough to demand someone tell me where my mother is.

(He spills a splash of milkshake onto floor and cleans spill with his sleeve. He smells his sleeve and then kisses cage.)

TIMOTHY: Wanna hear my design for DNA origami-based nanochips? I'll diagram it for you.

End of Scene

GYGES

Scene 7

Setting: Vivien's waiting room in day. BRITTANY sighs with disdain as she thumbs through a magazine. She discards magazine and repeats with second magazine. TIMOTHY enters, hobbling across room, gawking at BRITTANY. She sneers over her magazine. TIMOTHY looks away, struggles to kneel by cabinet and gather towels. He smells each towel and then his fingers. He struggles to stand and hobble toward door.

BRITTANY: You're Dr. Heifetz's son.

TIMOTHY: *(Still holding towels, staring at floor as he listens and talks, often shrugging.)* Uh … She raised me. Partially.

BRITTANY: She said she had a son who was … had a son.

TIMOTHY: I lived with nuns at St. Mary's until I was thirteen. They gave me to Dr. Heifetz.

BRITTANY: Is your last name Heifetz?

TIMOTHY: Daniels.

BRITTANY: Oh … Well, she said, "son."

TIMOTHY: You misunderstood.

BRITTANY: I don't misunderstand.

TIMOTHY: *(Pause)* I apologize. That was rude of me.

BRITTANY: I'm used to rude people.

(TIMOTHY sneaks a look at BRITTANY)

TIMOTHY: You dress like a magazine model.

BRITTANY: Lots of people tell me that.

TIMOTHY: Probably cause it's true.

BRITTANY: My left wrist is too large.

(She pulls back colorful sweatband on her wrist and

holds up wrist.)

BRITTANY: I worry when I dance—I dance ballet—people will be grossed out by it.

TIMOTHY: It looks perfect to me.

(BRITTANY pushes sweatband back into place)

BRITTANY: It's not. Natalie Wood had a large left wrist from an injury. In all her movies she covered it. She became famous.

TIMOTHY: Who is Natalie Hood?

BRITTANY: Wood. Really?

(She loudly sighs and dramatically rolls her eyes)

BRITTANY: She's dead. She drowned.

TIMOTHY: Oh.

BRITTANY: *(Awkward pause)* You're kind of cute in your own way, but yeah, a little bit cute.

TIMOTHY: You think so?

BRITTANY: I just said so.

TIMOTHY: No one ever told me that.

BRITTANY: I'm a good judge, so it's true.

TIMOTHY: How old are you?

BRITTANY: Seventeen. I pass for twenty-one at the bars when I wear my hair up.

(She holds up her hair. TIMOTHY briefly looks at her.)

TIMOTHY: Yeah. You look older—not much, just ... twenty-one.

BRITTANY: How old are you?

TIMOTHY: Twenty.

BRITTANY: Twenty???

(She laughs loudly)

BRITTANY: You look fifteen.

TIMOTHY: I'm twenty.

BRITTANY: I didn't say you ARE fifteen; I said you LOOK fifteen. Do you ever leave this place? Shop for clothes?

TIMOTHY: Dr. Heifetz shops for me.

BRITTANY: Your clothes look like something her age would pick. Buy your own clothes.

TIMOTHY: I hate shopping. I buy my software online. I'm good with computers.

BRITTANY: I suck at computers. I guess everyone needs one thing to be bad at. What are you bad at?

TIMOTHY: Being around people. Talking to them.

BRITTANY: You have that right.

(TIMOTHY stares at his feet as he shuffles)

BRITTANY: Do you have friends?

TIMOTHY: Perseus.

BRITTANY: What kind of name is that?

TIMOTHY: Greek ... He's a rabbit.

BRITTANY: A rabbit friend? That's pathetic.

TIMOTHY: We get along fantastically.

BRITTANY: Fantastically?

TIMOTHY: I have plans to make people friends.

BRITTANY: Then you need to improve your people skills. Hold your head up. Look people in the eye ... Do it now.

TIMOTHY: Do what?

BRITTANY: Look me in the eye.

(TIMOTHY looks at BRITTANY for two seconds and then looks away in shame.)

BRITTANY: That wasn't long enough. Look at me until I tell you, you can look away. Now.

(TIMOTHY pauses and then slowly makes eye contact. They stare at one another for ten seconds.)

BRITTANY: Keep looking ... Good.

(TIMOTHY looks away)

BRITTANY: Don't look away!

(TIMOTHY looks at BRITTANY and they stare for ten seconds)

BRITTANY: Good ... Now when I smile, smile back at me ... Ready?

(TIMOTHY pauses and gives small nod)

BRITTANY: Not yet ... Now I'll smile.

(BRITTANY smiles. TIMOTHY does not respond.)

BRITTANY: Smile back.

TIMOTHY: Now?

BRITTANY: *(Sighs)* Yes now.

(She smiles and TIMOTHY returns smile)

BRITTANY: Don't stop until I stop.

(TIMOTHY grins for five seconds and then looks away)

BRITTANY: Look at me.

(TIMOTHY looks)

BRITTANY: Good ... What is your first name?

TIMOTHY: Timothy.

BRITTANY: Then to not be a total loser, you should ask my name.

TIMOTHY: Oh, right. What's your name?

BRITTANY: Brittany.

TIMOTHY: What's your last name?

BRITTANY: I'm changing it to a stage name, so what my stupid family name is, is pointless.

(TIMOTHY looks away)

BRITTANY: Wait! Look at me.

(TIMOTHY briefly looks)

BRITTANY: You have nice eyes.

TIMOTHY: I have to go.

BRITTANY: I didn't stay to stop smiling or look away. Where do you have to go?

TIMOTHY: To put these in the basement laboratory.

BRITTANY: The basement can wait. What do you think of my eyes, Timothy?

TIMOTHY: They're ... beautiful, I guess.

BRITTANY: What color are they, Timothy?

(TIMOTHY shrugs and stares at floor)

BRITTANY: Always notice the color of women's eyes. That will get you far.

TIMOTHY: I need to go.

BRITTANY: My eyes are green with yellow specks, like the cleverest cat's eyes.

TIMOTHY: I need to go.

BRITTANY: Fine! Go!

(She looks at a magazine. TIMOTHY walks toward door, pausing to stare at BRITTANY for a moment. She does not look up from magazine.)

TIMOTHY: See ya.

BRITTANY: See ya? Whatever.

(TIMOTHY exits into hall. BRITTANY sighs, slings magazine aside, texts on phone. VIVIEN enters from office, looks at clipboard.)

VIVIEN: Miss Hickman?

(BRITTANY sighs, rolls eyes, and exits into office. VIVIEN follows.)

End of Scene

GYGES

Scene 8

Setting: Vivien's medical office in the day. VIVIEN talks while studying her computer monitor. PAIGE, sitting on exam table, sips from her water bottle.

VIVIEN: You had no headaches during your hour of monitoring.

PAIGE: I don't recall that hour.

VIVIEN: But hungry. Overly hydrated and starving.

PAIGE: I drink water all day. I skip meals a couple of times a week.

VIVIEN: That can cause headaches. You should eat better. The monitor shows you were listening to human speech. Was someone irritating you?

PAIGE: Evan.

VIVIEN: Patterns of sexual feelings and irritation are active. Perhaps you were sexually stimulated by a situation but did not like it.

PAIGE: You can tell that?

VIVIEN: Suggestive hints.

PAIGE: Oh ... Just before the monitor, Evan started to tell me about a sexual ... how to put this tastefully ... Oh well. I was asking him about a disgusting college sexual incident.

VIVIEN: Perhaps nausea too.

PAIGE: A sickening incident.

(VIVIEN intensely studies her monitor)

VIVIEN: ... And some jealousy?

PAIGE: You can see jealousy on your monitor?

VIVIEN: Infer jealousy. Interpretation.

PAIGE: I don't know.

VIVIEN: Perhaps someone flirted with Evan? At the office? Shopping? A neighbor?

(PAIGE shakes head "no")

VIVIEN: Perhaps it's an artifact.

PAIGE: You said your computer was accurate.

VIVIEN: For most parameters.

PAIGE: Evan does nothing to make me jealous. But he gets jealous. Sometimes it's like he becomes this other person: angry, jealous, scary. Wait a minute. The little girl next door flirts with him. Can you tell on your computer if Evan said a name?

VIVIEN: My program does not register language.

PAIGE: So, are you guessing like some carnie palm reader?

VIVIEN: I don't read palms. I monitor emotions.

PAIGE: You know more but aren't telling me.

VIVIEN: I'll study the results closer this week.

PAIGE: When we walk the neighborhood, that girl rushes out onto her porch anytime we walk by. Stares at Evan. Never looks my direction.

VIVIEN: Perhaps you have incomplete amnesia for the session, remember small bits.

PAIGE: Towels. Something about towels. Confusion about damn towels.

VIVIEN: The monitor registered confusion.

PAIGE: That little bitch.

VIVIEN: What do you mean?

PAIGE: The neighbor girl! All I have to do is think of what that girl looks like and I feel churning in my stomach, my face getting hot, sweaty.

VIVIEN: In your past, do you remember being bothered by jealousy?

PAIGE: Not this strong.

VIVIEN: Perhaps dreams mixed with memories. A side effect.

PAIGE: My head is starting to hurt.

VIVIEN: From our discussion?

PAIGE: If this crappy monitor is going to make my headaches worse, I should quit. Evan wants me to stop.

VIVIEN: All people have emotions they hide from view, but just the same, those emotions lead to headaches.

PAIGE: YOU don't have these headaches. Damn, this hurts.

VIVIEN: My assistant adapted our software for data to be sent through your phone. If we place his app on your phone, you can go anywhere. That will allow you more freedom and give us more information.

(PAIGE angrily retrieves phone from purse and tosses it to VIVIEN)

PAIGE: You're the doctor. *(A bit calmer)* I'm putting my trust in you.

VIVIEN: I'll have him load his software onto your phone. Will you be okay waiting in here?

PAIGE: I need to use the bathroom.

VIVIEN: The toilet is down the hall on the left.

PAIGE: *(Mumbles)* Toilet.

(VIVIEN exits. PAIGE gathers belongings, pauses.)

PAIGE: *(To self)* "Brittany." That's her name. Fucking little bitch.

End of Scene

GYGES

Scene 9

Setting: Vivien's waiting room in day. TIMOTHY loads supplies into cabinet. He does not notice PAIGE enter from bathroom and walk across the waiting room. PAIGE exits outside as BRITTANY enters. They barely glance at one another, however, BRITTANY sneers after PAIGE exits and quietly stares at TIMOTHY from behind. TIMOTHY finishes, smells the last item, and smells his fingers.

BRITTANY: Why do you smell everything?

TIMOTHY: *(Startled and jumps)* Oh. It's you.

BRITTANY: I have a name, "Timothy."

TIMOTHY: Brittany.

BRITTANY: You didn't answer my question.

TIMOTHY: Oh … uh. Some people trust sound. I trust smells.

BRITTANY: Now that's out there.

(BRITTANY sits, reads, becomes bored, and files nails. TIMOTHY counts items, pauses to stare at her.)

TIMOTHY: Nice day, isn't it?

BRITTANY: No, it's not nice.

(TIMOTHY stacks more items and tries to be subtle about smelling supplies.)

TIMOTHY: I found a chrysalis beneath our basement steps. Unusual to find a chrysalis.

BRITTANY: *(Still filing nails)* A what?

TIMOTHY: Chrysalis. Made from a caterpillar's under layer of skin. Turns into a hard case, not soft silk like moth cocoons. The pupa pumps haemolymph into its wing veins and voila: emerges as a butterfly. When my pupa becomes a butterfly, I'll carry it outside. Set it free.

BRITTANY: *(Bored)* Then something will eat it. *(Quiet as continues filing nails)* Do you have a girlfriend?

TIMOTHY: No. *(Mumbles)* I never ... *(Pause)* Do you?

BRITTANY: Do I what? Have a girlfriend?

TIMOTHY: Boyfriend. Do you have a boyfriend?

BRITTANY: Lots of "boys" like me. What I need is a "man."

TIMOTHY: Do you have a man friend?

BRITTANY: "Man friend?" That sounded stupid. No, I do not. I want a man like the man who lives next door. An athlete. Unfortunate for him, he has a wimpy wife. She just left here. Hideous sense of fashion.

(She slips while filing and cuts her finger)

BRITTANY: Shit! I cut my self.

(She sucks on her finger. TIMOTHY opens packaged gauze and hands gauze to her.)

TIMOTHY: Here's a piece of gauze.

BRITTANY: I don't need your "gauze."

TIMOTHY: You'll get blood on your shirt.

BRITTANY: It's a blouse! Burberry.

(BRITTANY accepts the gauze and presses it against her finger. TIMOTHY stares at her.)

TIMOTHY: Press tightly.

BRITTANY: I know how to stop a bleed, Timothy ... Quit staring at me.

TIMOTHY: Sorry.

BRITTANY: Why don't you have a girlfriend? You're twenty.

TIMOTHY: You said I look fifteen.

BRITTANY: Fifteen-year-olds have girlfriends. *(Under breath)* Normal fifteen-year-olds.

TIMOTHY: Do you want another piece of gauze?

BRITTANY: I stopped the bleeding. Here. Throw that disgusting thing away.

(BRITTANY holds piece of gauze out to TIMOTHY. He cautiously takes gauze by pinching the corner between his left thumb and forefinger.)

BRITTANY: You're left-handed.

TIMOTHY: I have difficulty with my right arm.

BRITTANY: So that makes you left-handed.

(BRITTANY picks up magazine and reads. TIMOTHY stares at her. She looks up.)

BRITTANY: Quit staring. Throw that thing away. Blood makes me want to puke.

TIMOTHY: I'll dispose of it in the contamination box.

BRITTANY: I'm not "contaminated." Throw it in the regular wastebasket for Christ's sake.

(She resumes reading. TIMOTHY reverses direction and drops gauze into wastebasket. VIVIEN enters from office.)

VIVIEN: Miss Hickman? Good to see you again.

(She extends her hand but BRITTANY flashes a pert smile and walks past VIVIEN into office, also ignoring TIMOTHY. He watches BRITTANY exit.)

TIMOTHY: See ya.

(VIVIEN makes stern, frowning eye contact with TIMOTHY. He makes sheepish eye contact with her and immediately looks down and exits outside. VIVIEN exits into office. After a moment, TIMOTHY cautiously re-enters, quietly retrieves gauze from wastebasket, holds it in the palm of his hand and smells it. He exits while staring at the gauze.)

End of Scene

GYGES

Scene 10

Setting: Laboratory/Timothy's bedroom at night. VIVIEN is sitting in a bedside chair, examining her notebook with her back to TIMOTHY as he changes from street clothes to pajamas.

VIVIEN: Fragments of memory leaked through, otherwise the woman would not remember the towels.

TIMOTHY: What are their names?

VIVIEN: I can't tell you names.

TIMOTHY: "The neighbor, the woman, the husband, the woman's boss, the woman's sister, the mother-in-law, the husband's friend."

VIVIEN: You're stuck with that.

TIMOTHY: You know it's not a story. I know it's not a story. You know I know it's not a story. I have a lame arm, leg, and crotch. I'm not mentally deficient. Treat me like an able scientist. No more pretending.

VIVIEN: So confident today. I need an able scientist to "visit" a brain and report the sensations.

TIMOTHY: I'm a scientist, not a subject. I don't risk my brain.

VIVIEN: I had hopes university lab technicians would volunteer. They can't even chart blood pressures accurately. Your super scientific mind, your exquisite sensitivities—

TIMOTHY: —Flattery won't help. And I'm mortified of being put to sleep.

VIVIEN: I cannot sync your brain if you are awake. Brief anesthesia is safe.

TIMOTHY: No.

VIVIEN: I will need you to sniff the Nano-Chip-Two aerosol.

TIMOTHY: I have idiosyncratic responses to synthetic substances. And I'd likely wake up.

VIVIEN: So, you wake up. Journey over. The other person knows nothing.

TIMOTHY: But I remember.

VIVIEN: Of course, you remember; you report your findings.

TIMOTHY: No.

VIVIEN: You experience the world from inside someone else's body. Move that body. Feel normal body sensations.

TIMOTHY: I thought you did this for science. Not because it feels good.

VIVIEN: Strictly for science.

TIMOTHY: Not curiosity?

VIVIEN: Scientific curiosity. Learn patients' sensations and help them.

(TIMOTHY, finished dressing, climbs in bed)

TIMOTHY: For how long?

VIVIEN: Five, ten minutes at the most. The first time.

TIMOTHY: First time?

VIVIEN: Enough to adjust to the sensations. Then the second time—

TIMOTHY: —Second time?

VIVIEN: You will have scientific assignments.

TIMOTHY: Like what?

VIVIEN: Charting visual cues, sound cues, internal body cues such as how bad a foot hurts.

TIMOTHY: Smells?

VIVIEN: Smell cues. Sources of pain, pressure, numbness.

TIMOTHY: I have pelvic numbness.

VIVIEN: The body you will visit does not have pelvic numbness.

TIMOTHY: Whose body?

VIVIEN: A twenty-nine-year-old man.

TIMOTHY: I'm not going into a stranger.

VIVIEN: For you all humans are strangers.

TIMOTHY: No.

VIVIEN: You are my assistant. Or perhaps you want to move out and seek another job.

TIMOTHY: This is my home!

VIVIEN: *(Walking toward door)* You're grown. Make your own home.

TIMOTHY: Wait! ... Perseus.

VIVIEN: What about Perseus?

TIMOTHY: You sent a mouse into a dog. That worked.

VIVIEN: I can't ask a mouse if it worked.

TIMOTHY: Perseus is my friend. I trust his brain.

VIVIEN: Mein Gott. You boasted you were an able scientist.

TIMOTHY: I'll do it with Perseus – or not at all.

(They quietly stare at one another. VIVIEN exits. TIMOTHY walks to cage and presses his face against the door and kisses it.)

TIMOTHY: Sorry Perseus. I have nowhere to go. She knows it ... Maybe I'll call St. Mary's. Talk with Sister Agnes.

End of Scene

GYGES

Scene 11

Setting: Laboratory/Timothy's bedroom at night. TIMOTHY is lying asleep on the gurney with an IV attached to his arm. Perseus's cage is next to him. VIVIEN enters and gently slaps TIMOTHY'S face.

VIVIEN: Wake up.

TIMOTHY: Huh. What happened?

VIVIEN: You sniffed the aerosol and did fine. But when I inserted an IV for sedation, you fainted.

TIMOTHY: I don't like needles.

VIVIEN: You refuse to swallow sedatives—or any medications.

(She walks to the computer monitor and studies it. TIMOTHY stares toward the cage.)

VIVIEN: The nano-chips are in place and working superbly in you and that silly fur ball.

(TIMOTHY sits up and stares at cage)

TIMOTHY: We're gonna be fine, little fellow. Me and you. We'll be even closer after this. Like twins.

(VIVIEN approaches the IV bag and holds a syringe near the tubing)

VIVIEN: This is a mild sedative, barely enough to render you unconscious.

TIMOTHY: I don't like those words: "render" or "unconscious."

VIVIEN: "Help you to sleep." Are you ready?

TIMOTHY: *(To cage)* Are you ready, buddy?

(VIVIEN inserts syringe into tubing)

TIMOTHY: Wait, wait.

VIVIEN: Done.

(She removes syringe and walks to monitor; studies it again.)

TIMOTHY: I already feel it. That's not mild! There's a chrysalis near the towel hamper. If something happens to me I want you to ... want you to ...

(He closes his eyes and sleeps)

VIVIEN: And ... sleep. Danke Gott. *(Pause)* You're in that obese creature now. *(Pause)* Mild anxiety ... strong olfactory senses. Figures. You don't trust anything until you smell it. *(Pause)* Focused on vision. Rabbits have a blend of monocular and binocular vision. I cannot imagine.

(She pauses, walks to cage, bends down, looks inside.)

VIVIEN: Hi Timothy. This is Vivien. You have hideously filthy fur. Let me know if you remember I said that to you.

(She returns to monitor and studies it.)

VIVIEN: You certainly did not like my visit to your cage ... Ah, playing with moving your ears one at a time. I cannot imagine that either. Maybe going into a rabbit was a good idea. Okay. Time to come out.

(She walks to IV line and injects solution into line. TIMOTHY moves, moans, groggily sits. He looks toward cage.)

TIMOTHY: Holy moly. I was in that tiny cage!

VIVIEN: You were sensing the brain of a rabbit in that tiny cage.

TIMOTHY: I was in that cage! You were gigantic, Vivien. And you smelled bad. Pardon me. But you did. Terrible.

VIVIEN: So, you could see me?

TIMOTHY: Not straight in front of me. I had to turn my head. Just one eye at a time but I could see way behind me, all the way behind me. And there was no red. Not even that warning sign was red. And I could smell everything: the solution in your syringe, what you had for lunch.

VIVIEN: What did I say to you?

TIMOTHY: You made sounds but they didn't make sense.

VIVIEN: Interesting.

TIMOTHY: Having fur was cool, but my belly itched.

VIVIEN: Perhaps the tape on its abdomen is irritating it.

TIMOTHY: Apply anti-itch medicine to his tummy.

VIVIEN: That will make it feel better.

TIMOTHY: Thank you for both of us.

VIVIEN: See what we learned. What emotions did you experience?

TIMOTHY: When you walked over, I was scared.

VIVIEN: Typical rabbit instinct.

TIMOTHY: I was scared because you were big and I was small.

VIVIEN: What a rabbit would feel about a human.

TIMOTHY: You don't get it. Those were my emotions. Timothy's emotions.

VIVIEN: I beg to differ.

TIMOTHY: I don't believe you when you stand on your pedestal and lecture to me that you know your patients' emotions.

VIVIEN: I know their emotions.

TIMOTHY: Follow my train of thought.

VIVIEN: I need to analyze my data.

(She walks away and TIMOTHY pulls out his IV line)

TIMOTHY: Ouch! I hope I don't faint again. Hear me out! With your lab mice you recorded their emotions when they were themselves.

VIVIEN: I charted that.

TIMOTHY: And you recorded their emotions while their brains were hijacked by other mice. Your word: "hijacked."

VIVIEN: It is.

TIMOTHY: During the time that a mouse's brain is hijacked, you are not measuring the host mouse's emotions. You are measuring the emotions of the invader mouse. Same thing with you. You invaded another person's brain. The computer measured your, Vivien's emotions.

VIVIEN: I was inside another person's perceptions, in her situation. I felt her emotions.

TIMOTHY: No! You felt Dr. Heifetz's emotions. It was Dr. Heifetz's history that bubbled up to create the emotions on your monitor. Like my emotions bubbled up when I was in Perseus.

VIVIEN: I extrapolated what she was feeling.

TIMOTHY: Extrapolation is not accurate!

VIVIEN: You have no idea what you are talking about.

TIMOTHY: Allow this woman's memories, her history to wash over you. That would be scientific.

VIVIEN: I won't allow anyone's memories to enter my own being.

TIMOTHY: You would if you were a true scientist.

(VIVIEN pauses to think about it for a rather long moment)

VIVIEN: Perhaps ... If we altered the signal portal.

TIMOTHY: We can do that.

VIVIEN: No. No. Too risky.

TIMOTHY: Ten minutes.

VIVIEN: No.

TIMOTHY: Five minutes.

VIVIEN: Still too risky.

TIMOTHY: You risked me and Perseus.

VIVIEN: Someday some other scientists can do that.

TIMOTHY: Try it with your animals: your mice, your chimpanzees.

VIVIEN: I tried that. Once.

TIMOTHY: And?

VIVIEN: I immersed a mouse in the memories of another mouse.

TIMOTHY: And?

VIVIEN: *(Pause)* Within one minute ... the mouse chewed off its own foot.

TIMOTHY: Why would it do that?

VIVIEN: I can't ask a mouse.

TIMOTHY: On the computer you saw what it felt.

VIVIEN: Fear ... Off the scale.

(They stare at one another for a moment)

VIVIEN: I need your help to create an odorless white powder containing our chips.

TIMOTHY: Powder can't cross the blood-brain barrier.

VIVIEN: Once mucous dampens the powder, the freed gold nano-chips will cross.

TIMOTHY: People won't agree to sniff powder.

VIVIEN: Drug users beg to sniff powder.

TIMOTHY: Not containing nanochips. Oh ... They won't know they're snorting chips.

VIVIEN: It would be unethical to not tell them.

TIMOTHY: I'm not taking part in any more of your research.

VIVIEN: I found a lab technician: Alexander. Super bright.

Experienced. I cannot afford to pay Alexander and support your living here at the same time.

TIMOTHY: *(Pause)* I don't have any place to go.

VIVIEN: Take your rabbit. Wait on the sidewalk for your fantastical dream mother to rescue you. It will be an interesting world for a young man whose only friend is a rabbit. Your choice.

TIMOTHY: That's not a choice.

VIVIEN: You're not accustomed to making difficult choices. Welcome to how that feels.

(She exits. TIMOTHY sits stunned for a moment and leans his head on the cage.)

TIMOTHY: Perseus, I need to find my mother. Now. *(Pause)* I am no longer thinking about calling Sister Agnes; I am damn well calling her.

(He walks to landline phone and calls)

TIMOTHY: I'd like to speak with Sister Agnes, please … Thank you ... See Perseus, I am capable of making difficult choices—Oh. Hello. Sister Agnes? This is Timothy Daniels, ward of Dr. Vivien ... YES! Wonderful to hear your voice too. I am so sorry to bother you, but I need your advice. Need your help.

INTERMISSION

GYGES

ACT TWO - Scene 12

Setting: Laboratory/Timothy's bedroom at night. Perseus's cage is on a stool. A dog is asleep under a sheet on a gurney. VIVIEN and TIMOTHY are both sitting and studying the same monitor. TIMOTHY adjusts a dial.

VIVIEN: Adjust the contrast so the nano-chip signal to background ratio is higher.

TIMOTHY: I can see a difference.

VIVIEN: You have young eyes.

TIMOTHY: Do you think the powder will take hold in Lionel's brain?

VIVIEN: Observe for spikes.

(TIMOTHY walks to gurney, peeps beneath sheet, and lifts his right hand with left hand as if in prayer. He performs the Catholic sign of the cross with his left hand. VIVIEN rolls her eyes.)

TIMOTHY: Maybe I gave Lionel too much powder. Poor pup.

VIVIEN: I warned you not to name lab animals; you'll attach to them.

TIMOTHY: Cause you hate pets doesn't mean I have to.

VIVIEN: Unfortunately, the dog's bloodstream will absorb some chips. Perhaps some into the gut.

TIMOTHY: Those chips will be eliminated. All that matters is how many make it to his brain and—

VIVIEN:—There's a spike.

TIMOTHY: *(Studies a moment)* Could be artifact.

VIVIEN: *(Pause)* Another brain spike. Your powder is working.

TIMOTHY: Too early to tell. Did you name the chips?

VIVIEN: "Gyges." "Gyges One" for the hosts, "Gyges Two" for the hosters.

TIMOTHY: Not "hijackers," or "invaders." Wait! Gyges? Like Plato's magic ring? The ring the shepherd found?

VIVIEN: Made people invisible. Appropriate name, don't you think?

TIMOTHY: Your chips permit people to perceive someone else from within. Not become invisible.

VIVIEN: A version of invisible. What would you name it?

TIMOTHY: Well ... It's like flying too close to the sun. Doing more than humans were meant. I'd name it, "Icarus."

VIVIEN: Are you saying you want to quit? Alexander is begging for your job. He won't constantly fight me.

TIMOTHY: I don't fight you ... Four more spikes ... How are the woman's headaches?

VIVIEN: She has strong jealousy. Triggers headaches.

TIMOTHY: Dozens of spikes! ... Hundreds!

VIVIEN: This past Monday she told me her headaches began when she was nine. A family beach trip. She remembers lying in her bed in a beach cottage, crying so hard her head hurt.

TIMOTHY: At St. Mary's, I had a headache that lasted weeks. After someone poisoned my dog Oliver.

VIVIEN: The nuns let you keep a nasty dog?

TIMOTHY: Sister Agnes did. A stray pup.

VIVIEN: Maybe the nuns did love you.

TIMOTHY: ONE nun LIKED me. Only my mother would love me.

VIVIEN: What helped your headache?

TIMOTHY: I stopped crying.

VIVIEN: This woman's head aches every day. But only at home.

TIMOTHY: Does she have children?

VIVIEN: No.

TIMOTHY: Pets?

VIVIEN: No.

TIMOTHY: Seems like she would.

VIVIEN: Not everyone wants children and pets.

TIMOTHY: Like you.

VIVIEN: That's a terrible thing to say … There was a man I loved. Mason. We had a cat. I wanted children with Mason. In fact, I quit taking my birth control pills— Didn't tell him.

TIMOTHY: More than I need to know.

VIVIEN: Like you, Mason was a genius. Eyes remarkably like yours. It was easy to lose myself looking into his … Well.

TIMOTHY: What happened?

VIVIEN: He died.

TIMOTHY: Oh …You told me a story about a friend killed in a plane crash.

VIVIEN: I never told you that.

TIMOTHY: When I first moved here. You said a friend died in Cambodia.

VIVIEN: Guess I did. He was on a jungle-temple expedition.

TIMOTHY: Hard to believe you had a friend who actually went on adventures.

VIVIEN: Why is that difficult to believe?

TIMOTHY: You're phobic of grocery shopping.

VIVIEN: Less than you.

(TIMOTHY hangs his head low. VIVIEN feels bad for her comment.)

VIVIEN: *(Pause)* Mason was quite romantic.

TIMOTHY: Did he want kids?

VIVIEN: He wanted to change the face of the world through science. Then have children. He initiated this project. We're realizing his dream.

TIMOTHY: You could have had children with someone else.

VIVIEN: Doesn't work that way.

TIMOTHY: You drive forward no matter what. Demand. Command.

(VIVIEN stares down TIMOTHY and then looks at monitor)

VIVIEN: Look. Thousands.

TIMOTHY: *(Pause)* Gazillions. Holy moly.

VIVIEN: Your Gyges powder is ingenious, Timothy Daniels.

TIMOTHY: Someone can sniff my powder and you can help them.

VIVIEN: More than that. I can help you. You now have an opportunity to visit a man's brain.

TIMOTHY: I would never go into another person's brain.

VIVIEN: Fear and doubt are written all over your face. felt the same. That's healthy. I

TIMOTHY: I'm not you.

VIVIEN: None of us know about the unknown in advance. Adventure. Mystery. Answers.

TIMOTHY: What if I learned about what I've been missing? That could be hell.

VIVIEN: Wishes and fears. Delicate balancing act. Picture this. You could be first in history to enter a highly healthy body as a person who lacks certain movements, lacks certain sensations. No one anywhere has accomplished that.

TIMOTHY: Who is the man?

VIVIEN: My patient's husband. He has a tingling foot. I would need to instruct you about this couple's house, details about the couple.

TIMOTHY: Why would he sniff my Gyges powder?

VIVIEN: He sniffs powder every day.

TIMOTHY: A drug addict?—You're not going to tell him. You're going to trick him.

VIVIEN: You would need to learn to take the bus on your own.

TIMOTHY: No, no, no. No buses.

VIVIEN: I have a program to override your bus phobia, desensitize you.

TIMOTHY: You already planned everything.

VIVIEN: Meanwhile, I plan to act on your suggestion: venture into this woman's memories—Just for two minutes.

TIMOTHY: Even the mouse couldn't handle one minute.

VIVIEN: I need you to alter the timer so the portal functions change after two minutes. *(Handing compact disc to TIMOTHY)* You need to begin this bus desensitization program.

TIMOTHY: I hope you chew off your own foot.

VIVIEN: More likely, I'll chew off everyone else's feet.

(She pats TIMOTHY on top of head and exits. TIMOTHY talks to cage.)

TIMOTHY: Perseus? Vivien scares me. She'll go into someone's brain and make them step in the path of a giant FedEx Truck. Just to see how it felt. "For science."

(He leans his head on the cage)

TIMOTHY: But I would like to know how a healthy body feels. Even if for a moment.

End of Scene

GYGES

Scene 13

Setting: Evan and Paige's living room at night. EVAN guzzles a mixed drink while PAIGE places her phone near the couch and checks it is working. She angrily arranges pillows on the couch.

EVAN: Calm down. You'll shred your "designer" pillows … You're wrong. I have no interest in the little twat next door.

PAIGE: Visiting my sister has nothing to do with your "little twat." I promised Amanda when she had her C-section I would be there. Sister pinky promise. Anthony is deployed and Amanda doesn't want mom and dad there. Who would?

EVAN: *(Whines)* An entire week is ridiculous. You might as well move in with her.

PAIGE: Could you possibly sound more like a four-year-old? I stuffed the fridge with easy-bake foods. Or eat out. You said eating out was better than my cooking.

(She swallows a pill and lies on couch)

EVAN: What are you doing?

PAIGE: It's nine o'clock. I need to relax. Another session before I leave town.

EVAN: Fuck! We talked about this.

PAIGE: You talked about this.

EVAN: That bullshit thing can't help.

PAIGE: I'm having fewer headaches. Dr. Heifetz and I talk about my emotions. Memories came back about the start of my headaches. When I was at the beach and caught Dad having an affair.

EVAN: YOUR father?

PAIGE: I was nine.

EVAN: YOUR father? He's ugly as sin.

PAIGE: You're talking about my father.

EVAN: Amanda's the one who pointed out the gross growths on his neck.

PAIGE: He didn't have them when we were young.

EVAN: His photos. He was always ugly.

(Audio: Phone ringing)

PAIGE: *(Answering mobile)* Hello ... Dr. Heifetz. Yes. I'm preparing now ... Evan is just leaving. On second thought, I'll move to our bedroom. Give me a moment ... Okay. I will.

(She exits. EVAN plops down on the couch, turns on the TV with the remote control, guzzles his drink, and lays the empty glass aside. He falls asleep.)

(Lights: Lights dim except for bright flicker of TV)

(Audio: After a moment the doorbell rings. A moment later, the doorbell rings again.)

(Lights: Return to full.)

(EVAN wakes, groans, sleepily rises, and answers the door. It's TIMOTHY.)

EVAN: Yeah?

TIMOTHY: I have a package for Mrs. Buchanan.

EVAN: This late?

TIMOTHY: From Dr. Heifetz.

EVAN: Of course, it is. Mrs. Buchanan's asleep. I'll give it to her tomorrow.

(He reaches for the package, but TIMOTHY holds it out of reach)

TIMOTHY: It's medicine. She's supposed to take it during her session tonight. It's essential.

EVAN: She took her medicine.

TIMOTHY: Uh … an additional medicine.

EVAN: Fucking head crap. I'll wake her and give it to her.

TIMOTHY: Dr. Heifetz insisted I give it and the instructions directly to Mrs. Buchanan.

EVAN: Shit. Make yourself at home. I'll drag her in here.

(TIMOTHY enters. EVAN pauses to watch TIMOTHY limp across the room. EVAN exits to the bedroom. TIMOTHY limps to photographs on wall and studies them. EVAN returns.)

EVAN: I woke her. She's "disoriented." Gets a weird accent.

TIMOTHY: You have a ton of photographs.

EVAN: Yeah.

TIMOTHY: You were on the swim team.

EVAN: Yeah.

TIMOTHY: AND the gymnastic team.

EVAN: Yep.

TIMOTHY: Wow! And in the army!

EVAN: Special Ops.

TIMOTHY: What kind of knife is that?

EVAN: Spyderco. Like a over-sized pocket knife.

TIMOTHY: Over-sized? You aren't kidding.

(He turns and looks at EVAN)

TIMOTHY: You still look in great shape.

EVAN: Yeah, uh, why don't you have a seat? Our photos are personal.

TIMOTHY: Oh, sure.

(He sits as EVAN waits in awkward quiet)

EVAN: Can I get you a glass of water? Piece of candy?

TIMOTHY: Uh, no thank you.

(EVAN paces and squirms. PAIGE enters.)

PAIGE: *(Slight German accent)* Oh. Timothy. Thank you for bringing my medicine.

TIMOTHY: Hi uh, Mrs. Buchanan. Nice to meet you.

PAIGE: Evan, this is Dr. Heifetz's assistant.

EVAN: I gather that.

PAIGE: Can you get him a glass of water? He came all the way here by bus.

EVAN: He said he didn't want ... Whatever.

(He exits to kitchen.)

PAIGE: Mein Gott. You only left me with fifteen minutes.

TIMOTHY: I wasn't sure that was you. You're gorgeous!

(PAIGE snaps her fingers and TIMOTHY hands her the package.)

TIMOTHY: The bus was late.

PAIGE: I tried calling you.

TIMOTHY: I forgot the phone.

VIVIEN: Mein Gott. I have to mix the powder and cocaine and install the phone app.

(EVAN enters with water and gives to TIMOTHY, who gulps it, spills a bit, and wipes it up with his sleeve while talking.) You have a lovely house. Very cozy, Mr. Buchanan.

EVAN: Paige and I are kind of busy here.

TIMOTHY: Oh, sorry sir. Thank you. Sorry to bother you.

(EVAN opens door for TIMOTHY to leave, but TIMOTHY stands motionless)

TIMOTHY: Nice to meet you Mrs. Buchanan. You too, Mr. Buchanan.

(EVAN nods to TIMOTHY and then toward door to

again encourage him to leave)

TIMOTHY: Oh. Guess I should go.

(He exits.)

EVAN: What a creepy retard.

PAIGE: He's very kind, helpful.

EVAN: Of course, you'd think so. You rescued the one dog in the pound with three legs—How did you know he took the bus?

PAIGE: He told me at the clinic he was learning to use the bus system.

EVAN: He acted like you two just met.

PAIGE: He was nervous. We met at the clinic.

(Audio: phone ringing)

(EVAN looks at phone to see who is calling before answering)

EVAN: Yeah Keith ... Fucking fantastic. So that's it ... This means a bitch of a celebration tomorrow, buddy ... You know it will.

(He ends call and dances a small but excited dance)

EVAN: Yes! Metasci and Newhealth are merging. Mammoth bonus for me and the team. Damn I love mergers. I got stock in both.

PAIGE: Good for you.

EVAN: Of course, I wish I had more shares. Thousands more.

PAIGE: Buy more.

EVAN: Never joke about insider trading.

PAIGE: Time to take my medicine and relax.

EVAN: My stuff's a hell of a lot more relaxing.

(PAIGE exits into kitchen. EVAN looks at photographs on wall, compares his present physique to photos, and

poses in Atlas pose. PAIGE enters with two drinks.)

PAIGE: Are you posing?

EVAN: Stretching.

PAIGE: Uh huh.

EVAN: That nut case was stalking my photos.

PAIGE: He was not blessed with your health.

EVAN: Glad I'm not a cripple.

PAIGE: *(Pauses as she is taken a back)* Uh, yes ... I poured drinks to celebrate your merger and mammoth bonus.

EVAN: Damn. First time you ever celebrated one of my business successes. Sweet—Don't tell the guys I used that word.

PAIGE: *(Toasting)* To your well-earned fortune.

EVAN: Is it safe to drink after you snorted brain crap at the doctor's and just swallowed a downer?

PAIGE: *(Holding up drink)* Cranberry juice.

EVAN: You hate cranberry juice.

PAIGE: As Americans say, " Bottoms up."

(They toast and drink. EVAN coughs after drinking.)

EVAN: Shit! Heavy-handed on the rum.

PAIGE: You earned it.

EVAN: You usually mix pussy-strength drinks.

PAIGE: My phone died. Let me borrow your phone.

EVAN: Died cause you and Amanda blabbed all night. You two have all week to gossip.

PAIGE: All week?

EVAN: Don't tell me you have amnesia for that.

PAIGE: Let me have your phone.

(She snaps her fingers)

EVAN: I gotta call Jake. Give him heads up.

PAIGE: Insider trading?

EVAN: Fuck no. Just a hint.

PAIGE: You told me the exact details.

EVAN: Your brain is being zapped. You'll have amnesia.

PAIGE: I need your phone for five minutes.

(She snaps her fingers more forcefully and extends hand to EVAN)

EVAN: Jesus, Paige. Did you snap your fingers at me? Never, never snap your fingers at me.

(He hands phone to PAIGE, and she walks toward bedroom.)

EVAN: Wait! Come here.

PAIGE: It's crucial I call before ten o'clock.

EVAN: You'll be gone all week.

(PAIGE shrugs)

EVAN: So … It's been days since we, you know.

PAIGE: Oh, uh ... I need to call immediately.

EVAN: I'm loaded and ready.

(He grabs PAIGE by the arm. She resists.)

PAIGE: You're hurting my arm!

EVAN: You're my wife.

PAIGE: Your cologne is making me sick.

EVAN: Thought you couldn't smell. Come on. You brought me a stiff drink. I know you want it.

PAIGE: After my session.

(She tries to pull away, but EVAN pulls her wrist)

EVAN: I want you now, God damn it!

PAIGE: Later.

EVAN: I'm sick of your fucking virgin routine every time I get turned on.

(He pulls PAIGE even closer to him)

EVAN: Relax.

PAIGE: *(Yells)* Stop!

(PAIGE pushes away with force and backs away as EVAN continues approaching)

EVAN: What? You gonna fake one of your headaches? Cry and whimper like a little girl? Leave me with blue balls. Or you got amnesia for that too?

PAIGE: My headaches are real.

EVAN: Real my ass. We're gonna do it right here, right now on your "Cancun rug." You ain't gonna remember anyhow.

PAIGE: The medicine!

EVAN: You should snort my stuff. You'd be climbing all over me.

(He grabs PAIGE and tries to kiss her, but she resists. EVAN slaps her. PAIGE yells.)

PAIGE: I'm going to be sick. Dr. Heifetz warned the medicine could make me vomit. *(Grabbing phone and running to bedroom)* I'm not going to make it I'm not going to make it.

EVAN: Fuck! ... Bitch! *(Yells)* And bring back my phone! I gotta call Jake! Shit! Where's the rest of that rum?

(He exits to kitchen and re-enters with bottle of rum. He sits and drinks from the bottle. After a moment PAIGE screams from the bedroom.)

EVAN: *(Mumbles)* Now what the fuck?

(He tries to open bedroom door, but it is locked. He pounds on door and yells.)

EVAN: Paige! Open the fucking door! Paige?

(PAIGE enters, holding a bloody cloth pressed against

her arm)

PAIGE: *(Her normal accent)* My arm is bleeding. I don't know what happened.

(She passes out and EVAN catches her)

EVAN: Shit!

(He gently slaps her face)

EVAN: Baby ... baby.

End of Scene

GYGES

Scene 14

Setting: Vivien's medical office in day. PAIGE has a bandage on her arm.

PAIGE: I don't remember cutting myself. I took the medicine, lost memory, woke, and my arm was bleeding.

VIVIEN: I made adjustments. That won't happen again. How is your arm?

PAIGE: I have to take my antibiotic for ten days and return to have stitches removed.

VIVIEN: When do you leave for your sister's?

PAIGE: This afternoon. For a week.

VIVIEN: Let's hope your are free of headaches while visiting Amanda.

PAIGE: Did I tell you my sister's name?

VIVIEN: You must have. Report to me about your emotional life when you are away from Evan.

PAIGE: I don't want you to form a bad opinion of him.

VIVIEN: He forces himself on you.

PAIGE: How do you know?

VIVIEN: Your fear levels are frighteningly high when he is with you.

PAIGE: I'm afraid to ... afraid ...

VIVIEN: Afraid to have sex?

PAIGE: I can't be calm when he ...

(She shakes head and freezes)

VIVIEN: Look at me. There's no reason for Evan to force himself on you. That is wrong and will not be tolerated.

PAIGE: Doesn't make sense I'm afraid of him and yet get so jealous.

VIVIEN: Our brains experience multiple emotions at once. Complex. Is it only with Evan you feel fear?

PAIGE: He is the only person I ever had ... Sex feels dirty.

VIVIEN: *(Pause)* Do you and Amanda discuss sex?

PAIGE: I don't with anyone.

VIVIEN: When was the first time you felt sex was dirty?

PAIGE: Grandmother Meeks was ... religious. She instructed Amanda and me that sex was a sin. We used to joke she was a fallen Shaker—Shakers are celibate.

VIVIEN: Almost extinct. Did you have sexual experiences as a child?

(PAIGE begins breathing faster with anxiety)

PAIGE: I ... I don't think so.

VIVIEN: Your breathing is speeding up.

PAIGE: I don't want to think about that.

VIVIEN: Maybe during a beach trip? A stranger? The groundskeeper?

(PAIGE abruptly stands and backs away)

PAIGE: *(Screaming)* No! ... There's no way you can know that! I never told anyone!

VIVIEN: *(Calming voice)* Okay, okay. Relax.

PAIGE: *(Angry)* I don't like that word. Evan orders me to relax.

VIVIEN: I'll refrain from speaking that word.

PAIGE: Why did you say, "groundskeeper?"

VIVIEN: You wrote that on your form.

PAIGE: I would never. No. Never.

VIVIEN: You were stressed when you filled out your form.

PAIGE: I wouldn't.

VIVIEN: Let me get you a water.

(She gets a cup of water and gives to PAIGE)

VIVIEN: Nice cool water. Good for calming. Drink slowly. Breathe through your nose. Mouth breathing excites people.

(PAIGE drinks small sips)

VIVIEN: This is impressive how you help your sister. You two must be close.

PAIGE: I look out for her.

VIVIEN: You protect your baby sister.

(PAIGE is sad and nods)

VIVIEN: You are strong, Mrs. Buchanan. A decent person ... How is your head?

PAIGE: *(Amazed)* I don't believe this. You stressed me, but my head isn't hurting.

VIVIEN: When people don't feel alone with ugly memories, their bodies treat them nicer.

PAIGE: God I need that.

VIVIEN: I hope you and your sister Amanda have a joyful time together. I hope her baby comes out strong and healthy.

PAIGE: Even if this baby girl isn't healthy, we will love her deeply. Like you love your son.

VIVIEN: My son?

PAIGE: Timothy. During my last monitor session, I had a dream about a boy—Or daydream maybe.

VIVIEN: While on the monitor.

PAIGE: Eleven, twelve years old. He limped like Timothy. Couldn't use one arm. I peeped at him through a rail fence. Ivy around the base. I wanted to reach out, touch him. I couldn't. Then it was night. I was standing on the edge of a river. About to jump in.

VIVIEN: Into the river?

PAIGE: From a river walk. Bricks slick from mist.

Overhead was a pedestrian bridge. I stood under it so no one above would see me. I looked down into the water, held my breath, leaned out … but then I saw a woman on the other side. Silhouetted beneath a lamppost. She had her hand out. I couldn't see why. Then I saw a boy. He grabbed her hand. A game. She hugged him tightly and they squealed with laughter.

VIVIEN: Seeing them, hearing them stopped you.

PAIGE: Pardon?

VIVIEN: Seeing the woman hug the boy stopped you from jumping into the river.

PAIGE: All I could think about was how much I wanted a child. Why would I dream that? Imagine that?

VIVIEN: Perhaps your memories of Timothy here in the clinic mixed with your dreams. Strange things: dreams.

(She stands, cuing PAIGE to stand)

VIVIEN: Have a pleasant trip Mrs. Buchanan.

(PAIGE walks toward door, but stops)

PAIGE: I appreciate what you are doing for me … more than you know.

VIVIEN: Wait!

(She walks to file cabinet, unlocks it with a key on a chain around her neck. She retrieves a small worn book, walks to PAIGE, leaving her cabinet drawer open.)

VIVIEN: I want you to read this. My Grandmother Winkler gave it to me. Advice about sex. In German and English. Our ancestors knew a thing or two about sex. Sex can be used as a weapon. But sex can be most beautiful.

(She pauses to remember and then hands book to PAIGE)

PAIGE: It's so fragile.

VIVIEN: The cover is frayed. The inside is clear and strong.

PAIGE: I'll guard this with my life.

(She surprises VIVIEN by abruptly hugging her. She exits, leaving VIVEN standing, paralyzed a moment. TIMOTHY enters carrying Perseus's cage.)

TIMOTHY: I saw Mrs. Buchanan leave.

VIVIEN: To her sister's for a week. I want you to go into Mr. Buchanan. For a full hour.

TIMOTHY: A full hour? If you care for me, you won't rush me.

VIVIEN: This isn't about your selfish feelings. This is for science. Explore Mr. Buchanan's perceptions, but fiercely defend against experiencing his memories. As I should have done.

TIMOTHY: I saw Mrs. Buchanan's bandage.

VIVIEN: We each recalled memories of the other's life.

TIMOTHY: Enough to chew off a foot—Or cut an arm.

(VIVIEN pauses, freezing as she goes blank again)

TIMOTHY: Are you okay?

VIVIEN: Oh, uh ... Perhaps some fresh air.

(She exits without noticing her cabinet drawer is open. TIMOTHY approaches the cabinet anxiously, looking back several times. He thumbs through folders and pulls out a folder. He hears Vivien approach and hastily stuffs the folder behind the cabinet. He stands by the cabinet, trying to appear innocent. VIVIEN enters, looks suspiciously at TIMOTHY, staring at him until he exits. She closes drawer and locks it with her key.)

End of Scene

GYGES

Scene 15

Setting: Paige and Evan's living room at night. EVAN is sitting on couch, wearing a T-shirt and dress pants, shoeless, working on his laptop and talking on his mobile.

EVAN: Yeah Jake, way beyond what we fucking hoped. Stocks didn't just double; they raced up the charts. Smashed the sound barrier, dude ... Shit yeah.

(He ends call and stands. He laughs and dances a silly celebration dance when abruptly he pauses and stares ahead in a blank gaze. He becomes sleepy and falls to floor. He is out for a few seconds and wakes. He is disoriented, looks around, examines his own body, speaks in a Timothy-style voice.)

EVAN: Holy moly!

(He rubs his face and body using only his left arm. He stands, limps to mirror, and studies and touches his face.)

EVAN: Uhhh. Why doesn't he shave?

(He learns to move his right arm. He flexes his right arm and wiggles his right fingers. He studies his right leg as he slowly extends it and places weight on it. He first walks with a limp, and then tries again, walking with less limp. He stops, concentrates and then tries again, able to walk with minimal limp. He stops and then stands very erect.)

EVAN: Holy moly.

(He lifts left foot, shakes it, frowns, and rubs it.)

EVAN: Well, that's annoying.

(He looks around to see if anyone is looking. He cautiously touches his groin area through his pants.)

EVAN: Oh.

(He looks around to assure he is alone, and slides his

hand inside the front of his pants. He pauses and then feels his genitals.)

EVAN: Oh my ... Oh my God.

(He closes his eyes and takes in two heavy breaths)

EVAN: Wow ... Holy moly.

(PAIGE abruptly enters carrying her makeup case, still wearing a bandage on her arm)

PAIGE: What are you doing?

(EVAN quickly jerks hand out of pants)

EVAN: I'm sorry, I'm sorry, I didn't mean to do that.

PAIGE: Do what?

EVAN: *(Shrugs)* Itch.

PAIGE: Itch? *(Strange look and voice of "that's crazy")* Okay.

EVAN: I thought the house was empty. That you had left.

PAIGE: I forgot my makeup case. I told you that driving home five minutes ago.

EVAN: Makeup case. Right.

PAIGE: Are you okay?

EVAN: Fine. Fantastically fine.

PAIGE: "Fantastically?" Huh ... Don't forget Kate dropped off meatloaf. Put it on high two and a half minutes.

EVAN: Love meatloaf. Really love it. Especially Kate's. I know you'll have a fantastic time.

PAIGE: C-sections are not "fantastic."

EVAN: Right. Fantastic considering. What I meant.

PAIGE: I should get on the road.

EVAN: See ya.

PAIGE: "See ya?" *(Pause)* You're not going to seduce me? Jump me?

EVAN: How would I jump you?

PAIGE: Right. Just … Hm.

(She walks toward door)

EVAN: Hope your arm feels better!

(PAIGE stops, looks at EVAN, shakes head, exits. EVAN collapses into sitting on the couch. He notices the laptop, looks at the screen, and reads aloud.)

EVAN: "Metasci and Newhealth. Multi-billion-dollar merger." Well Mr. Buchanan, aren't you a bigtime player?

(He reclines on the couch and stares at the ceiling)

EVAN: Oh darn.

(He calls on landline)

EVAN: I'm in. It's stupid being here … I can move my right side—and feel it. But my left foot tingles. Annoying … Mrs. Buchanan just left … Maybe I will; maybe I won't.

(He angrily ends call and lies back on couch, propping himself on his elbows. He stares at his crotch. After a moment he lightly pokes his genitals with his left index finger.)

EVAN: Holy moly … Wait a minute.

(He holds up right hand, wiggles it, and lightly pokes his genitals with his right index finger)

EVAN: Two handed. That's so cool.

(Audio: doorbell rings)

(EVAN startles, abruptly sits up, looks around, and remains motionless staring at door)

(Audio: doorbell rings)

EVAN: *(Mumbling)* Way, way too complicated.

(He cautiously walks toward door, limping. He stops, stands erect, and walks to door with an over-compensating confident walk. He opens the door.

BRITTANY is standing at door, dressed in formal evening clothes, wearing lots of makeup including purple lipstick.)

BRITTANY: Hi.

EVAN: Whoa! I mean. Hello.

(BRITTANY pushes her way in past Evan)

BRITTANY: I saw your wife drive away.

EVAN: Mrs. Buchanan came back for her makeup case.

BRITTANY: "Mrs. Buchanan?" She's been packing for days. Guess she'll be gone a long time, huh?

EVAN: I don't know. What do you want?

BRITTANY: *(Seductive)* You.

EVAN: Me?

BRITTANY: You pretend like you don't notice me. I see through your little act … Nice room! Look at your pics.

(She walks to photos and examines them)

BRITTANY: Those ones must be your wife's. Tacky. She looks cheap. But t your photos! Hot abs—You do notice me, right?

EVAN: You have green eyes, little yellow specs. Like a clever cat.

(BRITTANY immediately pivots to stare at EVAN)

BRITTANY: You know the color of my eyes. Oh my God.

(She rushes to EVAN and immediately pauses. Nervously she slowly reaches out and lightly touches his chest, evolving into slowly massaging his chest. She unbuttons his shirt as he stands perfectly still, trying to be uninvolved, but is obviously becoming aroused.)

EVAN: Oh my … Oh my … I'm getting an inexplicable sensation down—Oh my.

(BRITTANY slides down to kneeling, rubbing and kissing EVAN'S legs)

EVAN: I ...

(He looks down at his own body)

EVAN: Aren't I too old for you?

BRITTANY: I crave older men.

EVAN: You should date someone who is ... maybe someone twenty.

BRITTANY: I don't want someone twenty. I want someone experienced.

EVAN: I don't have experience. Not even with myself.

BRITTANY: Oh my gosh. Now THAT is funny.

EVAN: Ohhhh. You bumped my dickey ... Oops again ... You sure this is okay?

BRITTANY: You want me to stop?

EVAN: Uh ... Maybe not.

(She unbuckles his belt)

EVAN: Holy moly! I feel like a volcano is going to ... Holy moly!

BRITTANY: Wait a minute!

(She stands, pulls phone from her purse, removes Evan's shirt, poses beside him, takes several selfie photos with her phone. She places her phone on the table and again kneels.)

BRITTANY: Now where were we?

EVAN: You kissed both of my legs and bumped my dickey. Twice. I felt that really strongly.

(BRITTANY pulls off Evan's belt in one fast, smooth move and kisses his legs again)

EVAN: Holy moly ... I'm going to explode! Holy moly! Holy moly!

(Lights: Abruptly to black. There is a pause of darkness and abruptly lights rise to full.

(The scene has changed. BRITTANY is gone; the lamp is on the floor; Evan's clothes are scattered about. EVAN is asleep on the floor, wearing only designer boxer shorts. He wakes and looks around in confusion.)

EVAN: How the fuck did I get on the floor?

(He stands, looking around the room in a state of confusion)

EVAN: What the shit happened?

(He puts on his tee-shirt and looks at his face in the mirror)

EVAN: What the fuck? Purple lipstick.

(He wipes his face, looks around, and frowns. He pulls out the waistband of his boxers and looks inside. He slowly lowers his right hand into his boxers, pulls out his hand, holds his hand near his face, examines it.)

EVAN: Purple lipstick. What the??? *(Pauses, frightened)* I think I was fucking raped.

End of Scene

GYGES

Scene 16

Setting: Laboratory/Timothy's bedroom at night. TIMOTHY is asleep on the exam table with an IV line in his arm. VIVIEN injects a syringe into the IV line, gently slaps TIMOTHY'S face.

VIVIEN: Timothy? Wake up.

TIMOTHY: *(Groggy)* What? Where?

VIVIEN: You are home.

(She removes the IV)

TIMOTHY: Ouch! ... Oh my God.

VIVIEN: Are you okay?

TIMOTHY: God yes. I mean ... Holy moly.

VIVIEN: You should feel like waking from a dream.

TIMOTHY: I hope that was a dream. Maybe I don't.

VIVIEN: What happened?

TIMOTHY: *(Calms self)* Nothing. I mean ... I could move my right arm, my right leg. Pretty much full range of motion. That's what you wanted to learn.

VIVIEN: Any sensation in your pelvic area?

TIMOTHY: Uh ... I didn't pay attention.

VIVIEN: Really?

(TIMOTHY shrugs)

VIVIEN: Was being in another person's body a positive experience?

TIMOTHY: My left foot tingled. Annoying.

VIVIEN: Did any of his memories break through?

TIMOTHY: Uh ... Guns firing. An army tank, I think. It was on fire. For a second. And building a model boat.

VIVIEN: What did you do during that hour?

TIMOTHY: Exercised my leg, my arm, right side. That felt good. Yeah. Good.

VIVIEN: Exercised for sixty minutes?

(TIMOTHY nods)

VIVIEN: Describe the sensation in your pelvic area.

TIMOTHY: I told you.

VIVIEN: You did not.

TIMOTHY: That's private.

VIVIEN: I'm scientifically curious.

TIMOTHY: Visit Mr. Buchanan's body yourself.

VIVIEN: Move your right arm.

TIMOTHY: I don't have to.

VIVIEN: I want to see if you learned from being in Mr. Buchanan's body. Move your right arm.

TIMOTHY: No.

VIVIEN: Can you cooperate minimally?

(TIMOTHY moves his right arm more than usual)

VIVIEN: Mein Gott. You learned.

TIMOTHY: Glad you're scientifically pleased.

VIVIEN: Move your right leg.

TIMOTHY: I'm not a lab mouse.

VIVIEN: What else did you learn?

TIMOTHY: That I should never have done that. Now leave me alone.

VIVIEN: Do you realize how much you and I just advanced science?

TIMOTHY: Good for you. As for me? I don't care. It's wrong.

VIVIEN: Advancing science is wrong?

TIMOTHY: Your method is sick.

VIVIEN: Something happened.

TIMOTHY: You forced me to learn what a healthy body felt like. Felt good. Mission accomplished.

(He walks toward door with less limp than usual)

VIVIEN: You have less limp. When you do it again, you will learn even more. Your example will be a miracle for patients around the world.

TIMOTHY: You're not hearing me. I'm done. Hire Alexander to nose-dive into your revolting work. I'm returning to St. Mary's.

VIVIEN: A home for children? At age twenty?

TIMOTHY: I'll be the gardener!

VIVIEN: There's more you aren't telling me.

TIMOTHY: I have my own life. Do you ever consider that? You don't even comprehend that as a possibility.

(He exits, re-enters, grabs Perseus's cage, exits. VIVIEN calms herself and calls on telephone.)

VIVIEN: Hello, Alexander? ... This is Dr. Heifetz ... Fine, thank you. I am calling to see if you are still interested in my research offer.

End of Scene

GYGES

Scene 17

Setting: Vivien's medical office at night. TIMOTHY enters and sets down Perseus's cage. He retrieves the folder from behind the file cabinet, paces, stares at folder, opens it, and thumbs through papers.

TIMOTHY: Holy moly.

(He reads a paper, slides down onto his knees, almost as if in prayer, and rocks back and forth.)

TIMOTHY: Oh God no.

(He cries, leans on Perseus's cage.)

TIMOTHY: I thought mother was good, Perseus. Thought she would come for us … She never will. See this? She's bad. Evil ... And I have her blood in me.

(He collapses, crying as leans on cage and pounds it)

TIMOTHY: No, no, no!

(VIVIEN enters)

VIVIEN: What's wrong?

(TIMOTHY does not look up as he holds up folder. VIVIEN snatches the folder.)

VIVIEN: Where did you get this?

(TIMOTHY points at the file cabinet)

VIVIEN: Did you read this?

TIMOTHY: *(Mumbling)* It has my name on it.

VIVIEN: I can't hear you.

TIMOTHY: I said it has my name on it!!!

(VIVIEN pulls out her necklace with the key and examines it)

TIMOTHY: When Mrs. Buchanan was here, you left the drawer open.

VIVIEN: How dare you! Those are confidential patient files.

(TIMOTHY stands and stares through VIVIEN)

TIMOTHY: And my birth certificate.

(VIVIEN is taken aback. She struggles to calm herself.)

VIVIEN: I have an explanation.

TIMOTHY: You abandoned your baby in a basket on the steps of a church.

VIVIEN: I was a drug addict.

TIMOTHY: I was a baby.

VIVIEN: I couldn't care for myself, much less an infant.

TIMOTHY: You are a physician.

VIVIEN: I lost my license. No one would work with me.

TIMOTHY: You cure drug addicts.

VIVIEN: I tried to treat myself. I sought professional help.

TIMOTHY: Did you look into my eyes? See I needed you?

VIVIEN: I did. That's why I demanded the nuns return you to me.

TIMOTHY: Thirteen years before you could look into my eyes.

VIVIEN: I was building a life, making a home for us.

TIMOTHY: You raised me in a petri dish. Tested your methods on me. On my pets. Private tutors so I never met people.

VIVIEN: I didn't want classmates taunting you like they did me. I selected top-notch tutors.

TIMOTHY: You fired every tutor who was nice to me.

VIVIEN: The world is full of evil people. I could see it; you couldn't.

TIMOTHY: Where is my father? Does he know I exist?

VIVIEN: He died before you were born.

TIMOTHY: ... Mason?

(VIVIEN is silently sad. She nods.)

TIMOTHY: Lies, lies, lies.

VIVIEN: I'm sorry, Timothy.

TIMOTHY: Is that even my name?

VIVIEN: Your father was Mason Timothy Daniels.

TIMOTHY: Mason. The adventurer. The romantic.

VIVIEN: I didn't plan to hurt you.

TIMOTHY: You hurt me more than anyone can repair. Bedtime stories but never goodnight kisses. Forced me into evil experiments by threatening to kick me onto the street. Whatever was convenient for you. Well, Dr. Heifetz, I don't need you in my life. I don't want you in my life. *(Yells)* I am not your son!

(He walks toward door)

VIVIEN: I did my best to make a good life for you and me.

TIMOTHY: Invading people's brains?

VIVIEN: I came into money. We can build a house. Not live in three rooms atop a clinic and a basement. You'll have a real bedroom. And money to expand our research.

TIMOTHY: YOUR research. How did you come into money?

VIVIEN: Stocks.

TIMOTHY: What stocks?

VIVIEN: Health companies.

TIMOTHY: The companies Mr. Buchanan worked with?

VIVIEN: What do you mean?

TIMOTHY: Mr. Buchanan's laptop. Health companies' multi-billion-dollar merger.

VIVIEN: I never saw his laptop.

TIMOTHY: The fuck you didn't. God damn you're wicked.

VIVIEN: Don't curse like that.

TIMOTHY: Fucking evil.

VIVIEN: *(Screams)* I am not evil!

TIMOTHY: Explain that to the police.

(He exits)

VIVIEN: *(Yelling out open door)* Timothy? What are you planning to do? Timothy?

End of Scene

GYGES

Scene 18

Setting: Paige and Evan's living room at night – the following day. Lights are dim with TV light flickering. EVAN, sitting on couch wearing designer boxer shorts and tee-shirt, drinks beer while watching TV and eating popcorn. BRITTANY abruptly opens front door and enters. Out of breath, she closes the door and leans against it. She is wearing purple lipstick and speaks in a seductive, silly manner.

BRITTANY: Holy moly, Swimmy Boy.

EVAN: What the fuck?

BRITTANY: I love the way you say, "holy moly."

EVAN: How I say what???

BRITTANY: Sorry I'm late.

(She removes her coat and hat and tosses them on the floor)

BRITTANY: I had to wait for my pain-in-the-ass mother to go up to her room.

EVAN: What are you talking about?

BRITTANY: Oh my God. I love those boxers even better. What are those? Little basketballs?

EVAN: Get out before I call the police.

(BRITTANY winks seductively)

BRITTANY: Tell me the color of my eyes. I love hearing you describe them.

EVAN: How the fuck would I … You're the little twat from down the street.

BRITTANY: Not as little as you thought, huh?

(She walks to EVAN and rubs his shoulders)

BRITTANY: Wanna do it again on this tacky rug?

(She begins removing her clothes)

EVAN: Whooooa! I am calling the police.

BRITTANY: Say "holy moly" for me. Like when I undressed in front of you.

EVAN: You're dressed like a hooker.

BRITTANY: A hooker? Fuck you.

EVAN: No fuck you.

BRITTANY: Why are you being mean?

EVAN: Better yet, I'll call your mother.

BRITTANY: What happened to the sweet-little-boy act?

EVAN: You need help. How old are you anyway?

BRITTANY: Twenty-one.

EVAN: Really? You ride a fucking school bus. Oh my God. You're wearing purple lipstick.

BRITTANY: *(Seductive)* You sure liked purple last night.

EVAN: Last night?

BRITTANY: And you sure as hell got off doing "it."

EVAN: "It?"

BRITTANY: Quick on the draw.

EVAN: You're insane.

BRITTANY: Why the change? Oh shit. *(Whispering)* Did your wife come back?

EVAN: She's in the bedroom. She'll walk in here any minute. So, get the fuck out.

(BRITTANY studies EVAN'S face for a moment)

BRITTANY: *(Yells)* Mrs. Buchanan! *(Pause)* Gee Evan, I don't think Paige will walk in here "any minute."

EVAN: Jesus.

BRITTANY: I had no idea you were into playing games.

EVAN: Dose of reality bitch, you and I never met, never talked, never "did it."

(BRITTANY pulls out her phone and shows photo to EVAN)

EVAN: Shit!!! You photo-shopped my image. You sick bitch.

BRITTANY: Not photo-shopped. Real and hot. Next photo.

EVAN: This can't be for real.

BRITTANY: Next.

EVAN: Shit fuck.

BRITTANY: It's turning me on, you playing hard to get.

EVAN: You're a slut.

BRITTANY: Bet "Paige" will thrill to this photo. Me on top.

EVAN: Give me that.

BRITTANY: Want me to show her all of them? Drive her away so you and I can be together?

(She holds her phone out of EVAN'S reach and protects it with her body as EVAN grabs at it)

EVAN: Give me your phone.

BRITTANY: No.

EVAN: I'll make this easy for you.

BRITTANY: Any way you want to play the game, Swimmy boy.

EVAN: Hand over that fucking phone or I'll hurt you.

BRITTANY: Promise?

EVAN: Sick bitch.

BRITTANY: A real man.

EVAN: I'll show you a real man.

(BRITTANY lies on her back on the couch)

EVAN: No ... On the floor.

BRITTANY: Oh my God. So exactly what I hoped for.

(She stands and then lies on the floor behind the couch, out of view from the audience. EVAN stares down at BRITTANY, takes off his tee-shirt, holds it for a moment.)

EVAN: Up on all fours.

(He tosses tee-shirt across the room)

EVAN: That's fine.

(He turns off the lamp)

(Lights: Dim as a super-bright white spot pops on, revealing TIMOTHY peering through a window.)

EVAN: Let's see how rough you like it.

(EVAN kneels on the floor behind the couch with his body out of view from the audience, but his head in view.)

BRITTANY: *(Hidden behind couch)* What are you doing?

EVAN: *(Yells)* Die bitch!

BRITTANY: *(Screams)* No!

(Lights: Dim room lights go to black, leaving only TIMOTHY in bright spot)

(TIMOTHY turns away, horrified.)

(Lights: Spot abruptly to black)

End of Scene

GYGES

Scene 19

Setting: Vivien's medical office in day – one week later. PAIGE is cheerfully showing phone photos to VIVIEN.

PAIGE: And that's Tiffany at age two hours. Not bad for a newborn.

VIVIEN: Healthy baby girl.

PAIGE: You should hear the lungs she has. Fire siren volume. When I hold her, she calms.

VIVIEN: Nice.

PAIGE: And Tiffany ... Day four.

VIVIEN: Look how much she grew.

PAIGE: Most babies shrink the first few days. Not my little future Olympic star.

VIVIEN: Olympic?

PAIGE: In Junior High Amanda and I pretended to be in the Olympics. Soccer.

VIVIEN: Lovely.

PAIGE: And no headaches. Not even at home.

VIVIEN: Good. How's your arm?

PAIGE: Stitches came out. Small bit of itching.

VIVIEN: Normal for healing. How are you and Evan getting along?

PAIGE: I ordered him out. I told him his behaviors were intolerable and that I would bring domestic violence charges.

VIVIEN: How did he react?

PAIGE: Like the wind was taken out of him. He's withdrawn, almost pathetic.

VIVIEN: Perhaps he saw you grow stronger and he

acquiesced. Is he still at the house?

PAIGE: He's dragging his feet packing. A couple more days and he should be out.

VIVIEN: How did you feel confronting him?

PAIGE: Relaxed. *(Laughs)* Now, I adore that word. "Relaxed."

VIVIEN: You're reclaiming yourself.

PAIGE: Do you mind if hang onto your grandmother's German-sex book for another week? Amanda loves it. Wow did we laugh. Light bulbs going off.

VIVIEN: For as long as you wish.

PAIGE: Did you hear about the high school girl in our neighborhood? Brittany?

VIVIEN: What about her?

PAIGE: I saw her come here one day. None of my business. She disappeared. Vanished a week ago.

VIVIEN: She missed her appointment.

PAIGE: Her wallet, her keys, everything but her phone is still at her mother's house. The police are there doing … whatever police do.

VIVIEN: I hope they find her.

PAIGE: Me too. Well, I didn't mean to take up so much of your time.

VIVIEN: You used your time well. Warmed my heart.

PAIGE: *(Pause)* That's one of the nicest things anyone ever said to me.

(VIVIEN stands and extends her hand. PAIGE stands and shakes hands, smiles, and exits. VIVIEN writes in chart. TIMOTHY enters, walking with less awkwardness, carrying a milkshake in his left hand and a juice drink in his right hand. Ignoring VIVIEN, he goes to computer, sets juice drink next to the monitor, sips his milkshake, removes external drive from his knapsack, and connects it to the computer.)

VIVIEN: Good morning. I thought you left. Took the bus.

TIMOTHY: I did.

VIVIEN: Where did you go?

TIMOTHY: Out.

VIVIEN: You were "out" since six this morning. Five hours.

TIMOTHY: I plan to go back out.

VIVIEN: I see.

(She resumes writing in chart and then watches TIMOTHY)

VIVIEN: What are you doing?

TIMOTHY: Updating a program.

VIVIEN: Which program?

TIMOTHY: A program.

VIVIEN: *(Pause)* Are you ever going to talk with me?

TIMOTHY: I am talking with you.

VIVIEN: Eloquently.

(She writes in chart, pauses, stares at TIMOTHY'S backside)

VIVIEN: Alexander begins Wednesday next week.

TIMOTHY: You told me.

VIVIEN: Just reminding you so you can plan your highly private life. Gardening. Whatever.

(TIMOTHY does not respond. VIVIEN resumes writing. TIMOTHY finishes program, removes drive, sips milkshake, retrieves juice drink from beside the monitor, carries it with his right hand, smells it, hands it to VIVIEN)

TIMOTHY: Your morning fruit blend. I added bananas. Consider it a peace offering.

VIVIEN: I was going to make my drink after I charted. But

thank you.

(VIVIEN drinks small sip and smacks her mouth as she analyses the taste)

VIVIEN: Fewer strawberries than when I make it. It's okay.

(She drinks a larger amount, sets drink by chart. TIMOTHY exits. VIVIEN resumes writing.)

End of Scene

GYGES

Scene 20

Setting: Evan and Paige's living room at night – later. PAIGE talks on mobile phone while stirring batter in a bowl.

PAIGE: It makes sense the police are searching for every clue. This has to be excruciating for her mother.

(EVAN enters with a backpack, a box of camping items, and a small tarp)

PAIGE: Uh huh … Heartbreaking … Let me know if you hear more … No, uh, he's … *(Whispering)* moving out. We'll talk at book club. I'm baking cookies … Bye.

(She ends call, walks toward kitchen, and stops. EVAN is transferring items to backpack.)

PAIGE: That was Kate. She's friends with Delores Hickman.

EVAN: Who?

PAIGE: Neighbor in the cul de sac. Her daughter's missing.

EVAN: Oh.

PAIGE: Mrs. Hickman told Kate the police are rummaging through Brittany's belongings at home, at school.

EVAN: Hm.

PAIGE: Downloading calls, photos, texts. See if her account is active and she just ran away. She looks wild enough.

EVAN: Downloading?

PAIGE: Kids upload everything to the cloud. I set out your chess set.

EVAN: Keep it.

(EVAN rolls tarp and stuffs it in his backpack)

PAIGE: You have tons more junk in the garage, the attic. Hockey cards, trophies. The model boat you and Jeff were working on when he died.

EVAN: I don't need reminders of my brother.

PAIGE: What am I supposed to do with those things?

EVAN: Burn 'em.

(He slings backpack over shoulder)

PAIGE: Evan? ... Do you know anything about the Hickman's daughter?

EVAN: Why would I?

PAIGE: Nothing ... I just, nothing.

(EVAN walks toward door, stops, talks with back to PAIGE.)

EVAN: Do you think people have thoughts in the back of their minds? So tiny they don't know they're there, and then one day they pop up from nowhere?

PAIGE: I know they do.

EVAN: The line between what you think, what you do ... blurs.

PAIGE: The night I cut my arm? Everything bad that ever happened to me poured out all at once. I couldn't tell where the edge of the world ended, where I began.

EVAN: Sorry I added to your unhappiness.

PAIGE: I hope you find what you're looking for.

EVAN: I get close to finding it here and there. Then the bottom falls out.

(He walks toward door, suddenly freezes, stares blankly. He drops backpack and falls to floor, immediately unconscious.)

PAIGE: *(Screams)* Evan!

(She freezes, stares blankly, collapses onto couch,

immediately unconscious. They both remain motionless for a moment. EVAN wakes groggy and looks around.)

EVAN: Holy moly.

(PAIGE wakes groggy, looks around, and rubs and examines her arms)

PAIGE: *(German accent)* What? ... What am I doing here?

EVAN: Holy moly.

PAIGE: Timothy?

EVAN: Huh?

PAIGE: Is that you?

EVAN: Vivien?

PAIGE: Mein Gott. How did we get here?

(EVAN stands. PAIGE looks at her watch.)

VIVIEN: It's eight o'clock at night. I was in my office. It was morning.

EVAN: Eleven hours ago.

(He laughs fully)

EVAN: It worked. It actually worked. I put a sedative in your drink. Ran errands. Five minutes ago, I started my new software.

PAIGE: You sent us both here at once? Something can go wrong at the lab!

EVAN: This is so cool.

(He picks up mixing bowl and smells it)

PAIGE: Insane. How long did you arrange for us to be here?

EVAN: Seventeen minutes. Smells delicious.

(He lifts his foot and rubs it)

EVAN: I hate this tingling foot! Makes me pity this guy. Not really. He's an asshole.

PAIGE: This is wrong.

EVAN: Shoot. I gotta get something.

(He hurriedly exits outside with a slight limp as PAIGE walks to door and watches. EVAN returns, brushing dirt from his hands.)

EVAN: I had to dig something out of the flowerbed. Place it on top of the dirt.

PAIGE: What?

EVAN: A Spyderco. Over-sized pocket knife. It has dried blood on it.

PAIGE: Blood?

EVAN: Mr. Buchanan hid it there.

PAIGE: What are you talking about?

EVAN: The night after you made me go into his brain? I rode over here on the bus.

PAIGE: Why would you do that?

EVAN: I worried something bad might happen. I saw Mr. Buchanan and Brittany getting sexual.

PAIGE: Mein Gott!

EVAN: Brittany screamed. Mr. Buchanan carried her to his car. She was limp. Mr. Buchanan hid his knife in the flowerbed and came back inside. I checked the car. Touched Brittany's hand. It was cold. Her eyes weren't green anymore. I'm making sure the police find his knife.

PAIGE: Mein Gott.

EVAN: Brittany wanted a man. A man with muscles.

PAIGE: You need to call the police.

EVAN: I just stood there. Did nothing. It's my fault.

PAIGE: Explain what you saw. The police won't blame you.

EVAN: I won't be around to tell them.

PAIGE: I'll tell them.

EVAN: You won't be around.

PAIGE: Why? What did you do?

EVAN: We're not going back.

PAIGE: This is not our home. These are not our bodies.

EVAN: We'll stay here … until we die.

PAIGE: You are making no sense. I'll walk—or take a cab to the lab and end this nonsense.

EVAN: You don't have time.

PAIGE: Our bodies won't starve to death in a few hours.

(She walks toward the front door as EVAN looks at his watch.)

EVAN: In twelve minutes, our bodies will die.

(PAIGE stops)

EVAN: In ten minutes, pentobarbital will mix with our IV solutions. Two minutes after that: cyanide.

PAIGE: *(Pause)* You're murdering us?

EVAN: Appropriate for criminals.

PAIGE: We're not criminals! We're scientists. We're revolutionizing—

EVAN: —Someone else can do that.

PAIGE: If you think killing us will change anything—Alexander will find my notes! Scientists—my university technicians—will steal my research notes. Claim credit!

EVAN: I sealed your notes in a metal lock box. Gave them to Sister Agnes.

PAIGE: The discovery of the century? You gave THAT to a gardening nun?

EVAN: She arranged for the lock box to remain sealed for fifty years.

PAIGE: Oh Timothy. This is not like you. You are always

cautious, always consider every consequence.

EVAN: Brittany had sex with me because she thought I was Mr. Buchanan. Because of me, Mr. Buchanan committed murder. Because of me Brittany died.

PAIGE: You did not choose Mr. Buchanan's actions. He chose.

EVAN: You sliced Mrs. Buchanan's wrist. You swindled the stock market.

PAIGE: All research begins with bumps.

EVAN: Bumps??? What about saving our souls?

PAIGE: Those crazy nuns still talk in your head.

EVAN: Bedtime stories talk in my head.

PAIGE: Mein Gott. You and I are going to die. This is not reversible! What? Did you leave suicide notes?

EVAN: I left a note for the police, describing what Mr. Buchanan did. Where to find the knife. *(Pause)* The chrysalis opened. I carried my butterfly outside.

PAIGE: No one will know of my work. Mason and I would have been famous.

EVAN: Brittany died! You don't deserve fame. You don't deserve to be remembered.

PAIGE: We deserve to be remembered! Your birth certificate. This is because I left you on the steps at St. Mary's.

EVAN: I never understood you. Now I do. The world ends when you lose the person who warms your heart, who warms your body. I lived in someone for sixty minutes, felt those gifts.

PAIGE: I didn't love Mason for sixty minutes. I loved your father for twenty years. After ... There were no mornings I could lift my head. No reprieve to lift my spirits. All I desired was death.

EVAN: Drugs.

PAIGE: Sleeping in gutters, under bridges. Letting bugs

crawl over me like I was a decaying corpse.

EVAN: Memories of my father should have warmed you, kept you alive.

PAIGE: Memories evaporate.

EVAN: If you're weak.

PAIGE: Waste your last minutes berating me. But don't pretend you understand. *(Yells)* You're setting back science!

EVAN: I'm setting back you!

PAIGE: Yeah? You know what, Timothy? You die, too. That's permanent.

EVAN: I want your fucking Gyges chips, memories of my father, ME, everything you created to disappear.

(PAIGE yawns)

PAIGE: Your pentobarbital must be filtering into our bodies.

(EVAN looks at his watch and yawns)

EVAN: On time.

PAIGE: Unnatural sleep ... Seventeen minutes. You could have given us a few hours.

EVAN: I meant to leave more time. I spilled milkshake on the timer. It stuck on seventeen.

PAIGE: You are your father's son. A clumsy genius.

EVAN: Will I see him?

PAIGE: Mason? ... I don't believe anyone knows.

EVAN: What will happen to Mr. and Mrs. Buchanan?

PAIGE: They will wake. Have amnesia for these seventeen minutes.

EVAN: I hope somewhere back in their minds, they remember us.

PAIGE: They'll do whatever they were about to do. Live

their lives.

EVAN: The police will find my note. Arrest Evan.

PAIGE: Paige will be fine. She's strong. She's good. Lovely ... Happy ever after.

EVAN: Shoot. I almost forgot.

(EVAN hurries outside. He enters with Perseus's cage and places it and a note on a table.)

EVAN: Goodnight, buddy.

(He unlatches and latches the cage three times, smells his fingers, and kisses the cage door)

PAIGE: *(Drowsy)* Once upon a time ...

(PAIGE pats couch for EVAN to sit next to her. He sits beside her.)

EVAN: We always tell stories together.

PAIGE: Our modus operandi ... Once upon a time, there was a decrepit witch. Too old to bear a child. But she did.

EVAN: She brought a boy home. He was thirteen. He hardly left her side.

PAIGE: God, she loved him.

EVAN: For real?

PAIGE: Every bit for real. The beautiful boy began calling her, "Aunt." She couldn't bear to reveal she was actually his mother.

EVAN: Because she was mean.

PAIGE: Because she was stupid. Tragically stupid. They lived in a small—

EVAN: —You and Mason made it possible.

PAIGE: Possible?

EVAN: For me to feel ... Thank you.

(VIVIEN yawns, barely awake)

VIVIEN: We don't have time to finish our story.

EVAN: The witch and boy disappear.

(EVAN leans over PAIGE, kisses her on the top of her head, sits, holds her hands, and stares at her face.)

PAIGE: *(Mumbles)* My beautiful boy.

(EVAN yawns, lays his head on PAIGE'S chest, and smiles. They both drift to sleep)

(All is still for a moment. Suddenly PAIGE wakes and pushes EVAN off her chest.)

PAIGE: *(Yells in her normal accent)* Evan! What the hell are you doing? Get off of me!

(Evan wakes and is confused)

EVAN: What? I was walking out the door with my backpack—

PAIGE: —Get out! Now!

EVAN: I'm sorry, Paige. I don't know what ...

(He picks up backpack and exits)

PAIGE: *(Mumbling to self)* Pervert.

(She locks front door, turns, sees the cage)

PAIGE: What the heck?

(She walks to the cage and peers in)

PAIGE: A rabbit? Where did you come from?

(She sees the note, opens it, reads aloud)

PAIGE: "Dear Mrs. Buchanan. This is Perseus, my rabbit. I want you to have him because you are good and nice. Please love him. He likes to be kissed goodnight. I set up a trust fund for him for nine-hundred-twenty-seven thousand and twelve dollars. The information you need for the trust fund will arrive in the mail." Yeah right. I wish. "Sincerely, Timothy Daniels. PS: Perseus loves carrot sandwiches with mayonnaise." Such a bizarre young man.

(She looks in cage)

PAIGE: "Perseus," huh? Guess I could like a rabbit— Easier than liking Evan. Hi there. What gorgeous fur you have, little fellow. Yes you do. Yes you do.

(She opens the cage, reaches in, and pets the rabbit)

PAIGE: So soft.

(She sniffs her fingers)

PAIGE: You smell really good. What shampoo does strange Timothy use with you? Huh? *(Bewildered a moment)* Usually I can't smell ... Guess I can handle making a carrot-mayo sandwich. Strange as that is. Stay put.

(She closes and latches cage door. She walks toward kitchen but stops and stares at cage.)

PAIGE: We gotta look after one another.

(She exits into the kitchen)

(Lights: Slow dim to black except for spot on cage, pause, and spot fades to black.)

FINALE

DC Fidler (Author)

A native of the North Carolina Appalachian Mountains, DC Fidler has combined a career in academic psychiatry and cultural psychiatry with a lifetime of playwriting, acting, directing, composing music, and teaching creative writing and the dramatic arts.

He studied theatre, writing, medicine, and psychiatry at the University of North Carolina at Chapel Hill, where he served on the faculty. He later served on the faculty at West Virginia University and also practiced psychiatry in Australia and New Zealand.

He began his acting career in outdoor dramas, summer stock theatre, and local films and television at age ten. He has written scripts and composed music for over fifty medical educational videos and his plays have been produced in community theatres, at universities, and in professional theatres in North Carolina, Virginia, Ohio, West Virginia, Alaska, St. Louis, Sacramento, San Diego, Los Angeles, Boston, Chicago, and New York City.

He consulted and appeared in educational productions for HBO, ABC, and PBS and performed in stage plays including: *Hope is the Thing with Feathers, Night of January 16th, Thieves' Carnival, Blood Wedding, Our Town, A Life in the Theatre*, and *Fool for Love*. DC Fidler is an active member of the Dramatists Guild of America and the Charlotte Writers' Club.

Fidler previously chaired the Video Committee for the American Psychiatric Association and served as President of the Association for Academic Psychiatry, promoting the use of arts in psychiatry. He was inducted as a Fellow of the Royal College of Physicians of Ireland and serves on the Arts and Humanities Committee for the Group for the Advancement of Psychiatry, co-producing a video series on the History of Psychiatry.

DC Fidler lived and worked with the Alutiiq tribe in Akhiok, Alaska, the Al Moqbali Bedouin tribe near Sohar, Oman, the Kalkadoon Tribe in the outback of Queensland, Australia, and the Te Tau Ihu Maori Tribes on the South Island of New Zealand.

He is author of the textbook, *Psychiatry for Actors: Building a Character Using Psychiatric Principles*, and author of the novels, *Boogieban* and *Wood Whisperers*.

Novels and Textbooks by DC Fidler

- Boogieban
- Wood Whisperers
- Psychiatry for Actors: Building a Character Using Psychiatric Principles

Plays by DC Fidler

- Voices in the Woods
- Guilt by Association (With RJ Casey)
- Three Diaries
- Sir William Bowlinggreen and Company
- Shiraz
- Anniversary of Miss Nanette Pringle
- School Children Hiding Under Desks
- Grams
- Camp Uni
- Boogieban (Two-Actor Version)
- Boogieban (Seven-Actor Version)
- Ahulaqs
- Elk and Wolf (With Travis Teffner)
- Santee Delta (With Travis Teffner)
- Celtic Crossing
- Stone Touchin'
- Daugherty Park Merry-Go-Round
- La Dynastie
- The Last Farm
- Gyges
- Begat

Short Plays by DC Fidler

- Persons
- Cruise
- Mobile to Where
- Oman Truce
- Second Amendment
- The Greek God Club
- Five X
- Microscopic Misconceptions
- Drone Guns
- Moon Bugs (With Travis Teffner)

Screenplays by DC Fidler

- Green Lights of Baghdad (with RJ Casey)

Musicals by DC Fidler

- Pied Piper (With Lauren Horacek)
- Healer Man
- Medicine Show

www.ingramcontent.com/pod-product-compliance
Ingram Content Group UK Ltd.
Pitfield, Milton Keynes, MK11 3LW, UK
UKHW021656190726
13853UKWH00001B/301